MATTHEW BALLEZA

What The Men Saw

Copyright © 2022 by Matthew Balleza

All rights reserved. No part of this publication may be reproduced, stored or transmitted in any form or by any means, electronic, mechanical, photocopying, recording, scanning, or otherwise without written permission from the publisher. It is illegal to copy this book, post it to a website, or distribute it by any other means without permission.

First edition

*This book was professionally typeset on Reedsy.
Find out more at reedsy.com*

Contents

What The Men Saw	1
otherwise	25
Strongman	71
The View From Pier End	97
Night Fever	116

What The Men Saw

Donny Capretti was a technician employed by a telephone company in Boston to repair dead connections across town. His job was climbing poles and untangling utility lines, severing tree limbs that fell across wires, and crawling down manholes and laying cables beneath the city. It was good, decent work, and he had been at it for twenty years, since the time he graduated from Salem State and came home to take care of his mother when his father died.

Now he was 42 years old, a worn, unmarried, overworked man, past the prime of his days. He had wrestled in college, and there remained in his face a remnant of the toughness he had on the mat, but it was blunted, washed-up. He lived with his Polish god-fearing mother in the town of Medford, in the same house they moved to when he was 12 years old. It was a cluttered, green, two storey house with peeling paint around the outside and a flight of concrete stairs in front that led up to a small, wrap around porch with folding chairs on it. Inside smelled of lemon oil and wood polish. His mother kept the curtains closed to preserve her good furniture from sun damage, and to keep outside eyes from looking in. Cleanliness and dimness dominated her keeping of the house, and Donny knew they played part of the long somberness of her widowhood, which he did not begrudge her, but accepted under her roof. The room Donny inherited when he returned had the same floral wallpaper and pea green carpet it had when it was a guest room so many years ago. Like most rooms throughout, the furniture and decor was untouched since the day they moved in. Except his father's belongings; some of which had been sold- the piano, the shoes, bar glasses, clothes- and others that remained; fountain pens, books, opera records, family albums- and were constantly being transferred from one room to the next, for his mother was unsure where they should go, or what to do with them. But she could not get rid of them. They made their flights every few weeks; part of an ongoing act of purgation.

After work Donny would drive home, hang his helmet at the door, and find his mother, Greta, sitting in her arm chair watching tv or talking on the phone with one of his two older brothers who lived with their wives in Philadelphia and Maine. She had permed white hair, a sharp nose, and blue eyes. She was a steady, solemn woman; not unkind, but neither excitable. When she heard him come in she put the phone on her shoulder and called out to him,

Donny?

Yeah?

I'm talking with your brother. Go get changed and let's go get a bite. I got tired today so I didn't make nothing for dinner.

Then she continued her conversation and Donny went to his room upstairs, took off his boots, belt, vest, and put on sweats and came down a short while later where she was waiting for him at the door holding her cane. She was wearing a long, black heavy winter coat. She had a brown one that was just the same. She had put on a touch of lipstick. They drove five minutes down the road to a local diner owned by a Greek family, the Kolinakisas. It was an old standby. At dinner she asked him what was happening at work and he said, with a grumble,

The company's under new management and they're trying to make me responsible for a group of guys.

Like their leader? she said.

Their trainer, more like it.

Well good, she said.

Not quite-

Why not?

It slows the work for one. And there's no raise.

Oh, still, that means they like you, to promote you like that- raise or none. Don't grumble, and don't worry about the raise. We have all we need. That raise will come.

I just don't like being in charge of them, the young guys. They take the job, but then they start hating it a few weeks in, getting lazy, and I end up doing the work better myself. They're two more heads to worry about.

Still, they need to learn, she said. And you need to teach them how to put a lid on it when it gets hard. You're a grown man, they're grown men. You've been at that job for probably as long as they've been alive, is that right?

Some of them, yeah.

Remember what I told you when you first started out. To just do the work, put your head down and keep your mouth shut?

He smirked. You've been telling me that for twenty years, probably longer.

Since you were born, she said.

She took a big bite of her sandwich and shook her head as she swallowed and wiped her mouth.

And look where that's got you, she said.

Yeah I've got the job alright, same old job for the whole time.

Exactly. Not everyone can have that luxury, because they run their mouths, they don't learn, they say something stupid and the manager, you know…

She scissored her fingers then took another bite of her sandwich and put it down and pushed the plate away.

Either that, she said, or they don't move, they don't lift a finger.

She dabbed her mouth with a napkin.

Both lands them in the same place.

Yeah, I know he said.

So then you train them. You worry about a raise later.

After dinner Donny drove his mother to the grocery store and she bought a bouquet of flowers to take to the cemetery to lay on her late husband's tombstone. She did that every couple weeks. Like everything else in town, the cemetery was close, only a five minute drive from where they lived. It was a quiet, shady grove with many tall trees. When they visited his mother handed Donny the flowers and she bent over picking twigs and branches from the foreground. Then she stood a moment in silence, spoke a prayer in Polish, and placed the flowers. Then they left, and before they reached the car she was already thinking of all the other errands she needed to run. The visits were brief and dutiful; as unsentimental as dropping letters in a mailbox.

It was her duty to visit the dead, especially in the season of her old age, when the furies of grief were behind her, and the anguish of her heart smoothed from the jagged shapes life had made. Her days were cool and imperturbable. She could look at a tombstone with unblinking reverence. Gone were the days of bitterness. Gone also were the days of romance, buried with her late husband. Life had little of it, and Donny knew that. It was the unspoken law of her home, which he kept. That's why he took the job, and kept the job, and stayed with her. What remained was the house, in the town where they lived, which was unenchanting but commendable, where the buses were on time, the thinly sliced roast beef on sale every Wednesday, and more than anything, Greta's sons, the living extensions of their father, she knew were faithful, hardworking, and thrifty.

All day for work Donny trundled down the streets in one of the white telephone trucks with a hydraulic crane and basket in the back that could extend and reach powerlines. Every day he and his men received a list of repairs to attend to - routine maintenance at stop lights, drooping cables, and fiber optic inspections down manholes.

He could not count how many holes he had been down in his day; how many 200 lb covers, each as heavy as a millstone he had lifted off and leaned against the yellow protection cage they raised at every site. How many rats had he seen running below in sewage containments, some the size of cats, or how many syringes had he found dropped to the bottom. He had seen it all. When he was just starting out Donny worked beside a senior technician named Phil for two years and Phil taught him all he knew. Phil was a good repairman, but he had a lewd personality and one day it got the better of him. The two were working at an intersection and Phil was complaining about all the latinos and blacks being hired as technicians. He said,

You know Don, these dogs come over here, they take our jobs…and I'm sick of it, every last one of them. My pay keeps getting cut because of it.

There was a police officer on watch, a black man, and he was close enough to overhear every word. He turned around when he heard what Phil said, and Phil, who was halfway down the manhole, looked up at the officer, nodded and said,

Yeah, that means you too.

He laughed and went down, and the officer stared as Phil sank lower and lower until his head disappeared. Later that day Phil was called into the main office and fired on the spot. The officer had reported him. Donny told his mother the story and she said,

See, I told you. Some guys talk themselves into a situation like that. Don't be like that. You want to avoid the same fate, you keep a lid on it. Like I've always told you. It's not worth it. Your father had the same issue. Thought he could talk his way out of anything. A couple times he did and it worked. But it stops working. It kills you. So you don't be like that. I hate to hear that story. You just do your work, leave it at that. And that's all I'm saying.

Donny had never been much of a talker, but since his father died he stifled excess words, excess feelings, even more than before. He channeled what he could not express into his work. To his advantage telephone repairs did not require much talking. He spoke only what he needed. There was something more about his keeping quiet, though, that involved his looks. Since he was small he had a gap between his two front teeth that he was dreadfully self conscious of. He got it from his father, and he never outgrew it. Someone in middle school told him he looked like a 'dumb, brain-dead fag' when he opened his mouth, and since then he was scrupulous not to speak too much or smile too long or yawn where people could watch him.

Sometimes on the job or at home, in the emptiness of a moment or passing between tasks, he thought of his father. His father was a passionate but dissolute man; an Italian, 'Tomasso', who went by Tommy, who had dark slick hair, and wore well cut suits, smoked pipes, and sung opera around the house. He was a banker. Later in life he was besieged by an irascible temper and could not keep a job, so he drank heavily, which killed him. He died alone in the house. His wife found him lying on the carpet in the bedroom. But there was an earlier memory Donny long repressed that foretold the way that it would end. He was about 7 years old and he had gone upstairs and heard someone calling out in a pained voice, a moan. His parent's bedroom was open and the closer he came he could tell it was his father. But he could not hear what he was saying, the voice was obscured. Donny moved quietly to the door and pushed it open and said 'Dad?' His father was lying across the middle of the bed on his stomach. He was dressed in his suit but his pants were rumpled up his legs and his brown dress socks were pulled high and his beautiful leather shoes were mashed at the heel, like he had stepped onto them. The laces were untied and dangling.

Donny walked closer and said 'What is it Dad?' The closer he came he noticed his father's head was pressed into the mattress. When he lifted his head, drool ran from the corner of his mouth to the edge of the mattress where his teeth were. He had been biting into the mattress. His father opened his eyes briefly then shut them again.

Who's that? His voice was strooped and ugly.

Me, Donny said.

Don?

Yeah.

What are you-
Suddenly anger filled his voice. Get! Get out! he said.
Donny backed away.
Turn the light off, his father said.
Get Greta, he said. Get Mom.

As Donny was leaving, before he could turn the light, his mother came and shoved him out of the way and slammed the door. He drifted down the hall, and decades passed, and he forgot just how his hand shook on the banister as he walked downstairs. But he never forgot those words, 'Get Greta, get Mom.' So strange and alien. Or the door to his face.

Overall he got along well with the young men who came to shadow him on the job. He was required to lead them through a training manual, which he found to be cumbersome and written by someone who clearly had never laid cables before in their life. At lunch, the four of them would buy hot dogs from the convenience store and sit in the white truck eating and talking. Donny would flip through the pages deciding what was relevant to go over and what wasn't. Then after lunch they'd go up and down the streets doing maintenance and checking off the remaining list of call logs, repairs, installations. At the end of the shift he would sign off on their training and drop them off at a pub in town where all the technicians in the area met on weeknights for a drink.

You coming in? they asked him.
No, no. You guys enjoy. I've got my mother to get home to.

Which was part true. The part he did not tell them was that he had fear of the drink. It was a fear rooted in the manner of his father's death, and two decades of his mother's doomsaying on the matter.

Don't let the same happen to you, she'd tell him. You're prone, just as much as he was.

Sometimes she would say it with so much conviction that she would sob, then pull herself together.

It's in your blood, she said. It was the only time he saw her like that.

Over many years her warning became an omen over him. An imputation. He feared trespassing her warning as much as he feared the drink itself. It occurred to him that even she drank red wine occasionally, but when he questioned her she said,

Donny, no. This isn't about me. I've lived 75 years with no issue. This isn't the same. If it was the same as your father, then that's different. But you don't hear me screaming in the middle of the night or being found naked in my car the next day. No. Our Lord drank wine, you see? He did not drink liquor. Those are two very different things. Don't try to be clever. I say these things to you and your brothers for the same reason.

Meanwhile he dropped his men weekly at the pub. Many times driving home he questioned his abstinence, but it remained only a question, and ended when he reached the door. He stuck to the foursquare limits of his day, the dry boundary between work and home. And after a while the men knew where he stood; they stopped asking him to join.

In the days following a tombstone visit, his mother's spirit would drop from its already low stature and she would ruminate on her late husband's death, and it would make her sad to remember him, and she became overwhelmed with life, and her old age, and her sons- especially the two she never saw. Those days she carried a wet rag around the house like a hankie, and cleaned every surface she came upon. Cleaning helped her mourn and the home smelled strongly afterwards of Ajax and more lemon oil.

Donny was careful what he spoke about, careful not to trigger something that would send her into a deeper rumination. But speaking of work was fine. Of all subjects, Donny's work was a subject she was almost entirely dispassionate toward. Although she asked him many questions about his day, she had little idea what he actually did, how he spent his hours in a truck and underground with work gloves, cutters, and a reflective vest on. The only thing she could picture was him climbing a telephone pole, because sometimes she would look out the window of their house and see a man fixing the power lines between their house and another. And when Donny would return she would say,

I saw one of your friends working on the lines in front of our house. You wouldn't happen to know him would you?

I doubt it. There's hundreds of us in this region.

Sometimes when they were watching the news together she would lower the volume and say,

Don? You don't mind closing his office door, would you? I think I forgot to close it.

A thought like that would come to her out of the blue. Or,

Don? Can you make sure his records get put away. I took them out for dusting earlier.

He would do all she asked of him. He was like an indentured son, and he was used to her way of speaking of her dead husband in the third person, as if the man were still around, present in his things, sparkling in a glass, or furtive in a footstool. Hidden and tucked. She was shy to speak his name explicitly because it had power over, calling to mind so many heavy and baneful thoughts that she went into a slough and could not be pulled out of it easily.

The whole house came under the spell. So long as Donny was there he found his own mind wandering back to specific scenes from his childhood. Times with his father. He remembered the times when his father returned from work and was caught with a bottle of gin. He remembered it so clear because it was his father's instinct to laugh when his mother caught him. His father had an uproarious laugh. He would laugh loudly and wildly and wonderfully, breaking into comedy. It was the way he disarmed his wife's unhappiness, how he chipped away at her imperious eyes. He melted before her. He was like a child who stole candy, who when found suddenly bubbles over with sweetness and obedience and neat resolutions.

Donny's mother would find liquor on him and ask him why he had it, and he would take it from his pocket and put it on the kitchen table for all of them gathered to see, as if to say 'Here. Here I am. I hide nothing from you. Even this. This was a test, you see.' He would cling to her and pour on the effects of his charm. The boys would be there watching. He would put his hand behind her neck and kiss her on the cheek, very affectionately, and say to her,

Why are you so stiff? Why my love? Please, relax. Relax for me.

He would turn to his sons and say,

You boys, you see? How beautiful, how very sharp your mother is. She sees my trouble from a mile away. Still, look how she loves us. We must always be good to her. We do not deserve her.

Then he turns back to her. She's leaning against the counter, resisting. He puts his hands on her shoulders and holds her out in front of him, like a great painting.

I'll take care of this my love. I promise. Boys? He turns back again. You see? But she struggles in his hold and tries to take the bottle on the table instead. But he pulls her hands away and brings them to his lips and kisses them. There, there. Ok? he says.

Here Donny, he says. He gives the bottle to Donny, the youngest, to hold. Again she struggles against him and she tries to take it from Donny, but he holds her off. He is strong and calm.

Ah, ah. he says.

Stop, Tom. Keep that away from him. I don't want him holding that- that poison, whatever it is. You have told me so many times enough. I do not want it in my house.

Poison? Oh come now, enough my love, that's too much.

He reads her distress, so he softens into more silk. He mellows his voice. He looks back at Donny.

You hide this from me so I don't find it ok?

His son nods.

Make sure I don't find it. You must hide it very well. He says this strongly and assertive, raising his voice. Can you do that?

His son nods again. He looks again at his wife. He put his hands to her face and holds it, like it was precious, looking over it slowly. The eyes he sees are blue and on fire. They avoid him.

Keep that away from him, she says.

He says to her, Look now, it's done. He wipes his hands in the air. Is that good? he says. What else? I will change. You see? He nods back. They can see too. I am changing. Am I weak? Yes. But no more trouble. I am trying. You know this my love.

He takes her hands, then releases them.

She reaches her arms around him as if to hug him finally, but she slides them into the side pockets of his coat instead and takes hold of another small glass bottle of poison and he grasps her wrists, but her hand is already clutched upon the bottle and he lets her take it out. She does not assail him with words, but with her face, her staunch, steady eyes, in the company of her sons who have not said a thing.

Oh, no, no, no, he says. He laughs again, but this laugh is different. It is higher and strained. He lets go of her wrist. She reads the label and he reaches for it, but she pulls it away and he removes his hands and puts them behind his head, in the gesture of arrest.

See, he says. I am caught. You do with that what you want my love. I should have known that was there. I forgot. I truly did forget. Am I allowed to forget? No?

She goes past him, out of the kitchen, out of the house, and he follows her. And the boys follow them, and they watch as she breaks the bottle on the cement driveway. The father says nothing. His face is sorrowful. The boys stand at the door and as she walks in past them, the fumes of liquor are heavy in the air and she pulls Donny in and tells him to cover his nose.

Go inside. Go. she says. Get away from that smell.

She returns to the kitchen and stands where she was, at the sink, and he follows her and stands in the same place too.

You had to break it like that? he says. You couldn't just pour it out. Now we have to clean it.

Her arms are folded.

Don't worry about cleaning, she says. She turns to her boys who are standing behind their father.

Get out of here, boys, enough for you. Donny put that down and go.

No boys. Don't go.

The boys stay.

The man comes close to his wife and takes her arms that are rigid and folded.

Oh what? she says. Come on, no. What're you doing?

She is resistant, but he forces her into the posture of a waltz. He is trying to play with her. And she twists and stomps the floor.

What? she says. Come on. I don't want this. You're making a game. This isn't a game.

No more, please my love. This is no game. Yes, you are right. I am at fault. I am the trouble. But dance with me.

Stop now, I'm not in this mood.

She takes his arms off and he takes her up again.

Just be in the mood with me. With your trouble. Remember our wedding, how we danced? With me, come now.

He tries to pin her eyes with his but they feign and turn, and then they meet; and then slightly, ever so slightly and unwillingly she grins. Then she straightens it again, but he has seen it already.

Ah, there, he says. There. Finally, something! Ah, hahaha, oh what is this now?

He holds her firm.

I can't hide from you. I have learned this many times. Come here, kiss me.

He kisses her. She turns her neck.

You know this don't you?

He looks back at the boys.

You see boys, your mother? How did I find her? How did I ever?

He releases her and stands apart, and he speaks to the boys

but he is really speaking to her aloud.

Everywhere I go, she knows, she is there already. I come home- she is there. I go to the store, she is there. To work- she is there too. I have a drink- what do you think? She is there, she knows. I bring home this trouble- she knows too. I can go on. You see her eyes? You each have them. Her eyes. They are always seeing, always seeing me you know. That's why we are lucky.

And he laughs, full of mirth and guilt. He continues with this charade, this dramatic, operatic reenactment of his love, swaying around her like a sculptor, and she his ton of white, immovable Carrara marble.

At times his movement and aura would seem to pacify her and she was more inclined to remove him off her than reprimand his drinking. Yet for all his outpouring of festivity, it was succeeded often by a sadness, a serious and almost Polish sadness that would come upon him- and he would go to Donny's bedside late at night, wake his son in the dark and ask him where he hid the bottle. And his son would tell him. Later, when the other two sons left the house, the father's sickness decayed into a rage that emerged spontaneously and was unreproved by any courtship or romance. There was no revelry anymore. There was only drunken anger. Bawling, gibberish. Greta would call her sons and say to them,

You are my strength, you are each my strength. I have none here in this house. Your father, no. He is wasted and sick. And so am I.

Then he died. But even after his death, and the bleak years following, when she and Donny all but subsisted in that house, she protected the dignity of her late husband whenever she spoke of him. She attributed to his death a sickness, not a shame. The shame, if any, was her own; it was the knowledge and pain of her futility, of being unable to rescue him from the brink. Early in the wake of his death she would say to Donny,

I was given so little in this life to look after, including him. And now what? I could not even look after him.

Then that feeling of crookedness turned to helplessness. and helplessness turned to indifference, and indifference fermented into slumber. And many years passed, one to the next, the hearts in that house put out; snuffed of living flame; stoking only barren coals called time and duty and family and the job where Donny drove around repairing telephone lines.

At the end of 6 months, the men shadowing Donny were about to graduate and be deployed to other parts of the city to work as self-sufficient technicians. Donny was proud of their accomplishment and confident that they were capable of handling nearly all of the repairs they would come across. But in the week before last, Donny's supervisor called him and said that he and his men were requested for a special assignment. Evidently there was a massive construction site sprawled over one of the busiest intersections in the city, and the foreman of the site called and asked for help with one of the manholes which had the telephone company's imprint on it. Donny's supervisor said it would be a good opportunity to show the trainees how to operate in a complex situation. They were given no other orders beside that.

When they arrived, the foreman sat off the barricade he was leaning on and went to meet them. He was a tall man with a white mustache and a clipboard under his arm with papers flying. Most of his men were standing by, loitering and talking. Another group, not far from where they stood was operating a jackhammer, which made a high metallic racket every few seconds- jig jig jig jig jig jig jig jig, and filled the air with dust. Bicycles and trucks and cars were honking and swerving around the barricades in the one open lane, and there was a police officer in a bright yellow jacket and tall black boots standing on the outskirts of the commotion waving people along. Laying across the ground in the excavation zone were pipes and fittings and moldings and stacks of rebar. The near sidewalk had been chewed open by a small bulldozer. But in the middle of the wreckage was a single manhole, with the inscription of the telephone company on it. Ten feet above the hole was a crane hook, and the crane itself, with its long arm reaching to the sky, had the name "Mackey & Sons" written on it, with the motto "Better building brings us together". The foreman showed them what was going on.

We're breaking up this half of the street so we can get to the pipelines below and re-plumb this whole area. The crane is ready to go in case we use it, but we need one of you to get down this hole to see what we're dealing with in case we break through it, or if it needs to be secured somehow. We don't want to damage more than we have to. This is your hole isn't it?

Donny said, I've never worked this part of the grid before, but it looks like our cover.

Yeah, that's why we called. We almost missed it since we were kicking up so much dust taking out the sidewalk, but the cover was propped open already.

You didn't open it? Donny said.

Course not. Not without permission. I told my guys we'll hold off until someone gets down there and sees it and oks it.

When did you start construction?

Just this morning.

It shouldn't have been open, but I'll go down there and see what's going on and these guys will help me with the cover and anything else.

Should I move the crane? the foreman said.

You can keep the crane where it is. Most of these holes aren't too deep that I'd need it.

Donny suited up and his trainees brought the yellow protection crate around the hole and lifted off the cover. One of the men plugged his nose and said,

Gollee, smells god awful down there.

It must be close to the sewage, Donny said. And get used to those smells, it ain't ever going to smell pretty.

The manhole had rebar steps that Donny mounted and descended while his men stood outside waiting by the crate, looking in. Below him was blackness. It was deeper than he imagined, in fact, much deeper than any hole he had been down before. Step by step he went. Looking around, he was certain it was not his company's hole, but he did not know whose it was, or what it was used for. It was far too deep; so deep he could not see the bottom clearly even with his headlamp. This was more of a mineshaft than a manhole. The sidewalls were brick, a material they stopped using long ago, and they were spackled in spots where the groundwater leaked. He considered calling his men on the walkie to send in the crane hook for safety, but he decided against it, believing it might encumber him as he went down the narrow way. Many feet below him was a metal landing platform that was drilled into the sides of the walls, for resting or staging tools on. There was another platform 8 feet below it. And beneath that he could not see. The lower he went the air grew rank and putrid. Above ground the foreman waited for his men who were sitting on the barricade beside him. The crane was poised motionless over the hole, and the jackhammer continued its demolition, hazing the air and spattering the street in rubble. The ground rattled, and Donny heard it below, like knuckles rapping on a door.

The men's eyes were transfixed on the hole. They had no interest in it, except that it stood between them and their labor. They were bored dumb, and after their glazed eyes wandered every which way, they returned and rested on that solitary blackness, waiting for something, they knew not what. One of the men called Donny on the walkie, and said

How you doing down there?

I'm fine, he said, but tell that forman this isn't our hole. I don't know whose it is. Maybe sewage, but it's old though. Too old to be in use. I don't know who's been in here. I'll check in with you in a minute.

He rested a moment on the first platform before starting again. When he got back on the steps the edge of the platform clipped his walkie off his belt and it fell all the way down, hitting the bottom with a splash and crack. He could see the water at bottom wrinkle with a gleam. He descended 8 more feet and made it past the second platform. Then he could see unobstructed to the bottom, which was another 8 feet to the ground. The space around him was tight, not more than two shoulder widths, and the lower he went the tighter it felt. Above the standing water was a landing made of three wooden boards, and atop the boards was something that looked like a table chair covered in a blanket. He was cautious, for he did not know what it was, and the closer he stepped to the bottom the hair on his neck stood on end, for the figure he saw looked less and less like a chair and more like a hunched body, though covered and obscured and unmoving. No, he said. Impossible. No one would come down here.

When his feet touched the landing he tested the footing and the boards creaked as he turned around slowly. His headlamp was on and within seconds he saw what most he feared. The shoulders and the neck and the knees of a body. Knees drawn to the chest, like the seat of a chair. The blanket around it was blue with rainbow trim. A shudder of fear seized him and he felt it in his stomach. He yelled above, his voice echoing up through the shaft,

Hey!

One of his men came and stuck his head over the hole and called down.

Don, everything alright?

Get the foreman, he yelled back. That was all he said. The man left to get the foreman and Donny's hands were trembling uncontrollably. and he tried to still the trembling by clenching his hands tightly, then releasing them. He could feel himself swallow, and even his swallow he tried to slow, to lessen. He could taste bile at the back of his throat. He removed his helmet and placed it at his feet with the lamp still shining forward on the object. Then, very gently he reached out and put his hand on the shoulder of the body, the body he knew was dead the moment he touched it. He turned it slowly, away from the wall where it leaned, toward him, at the same time removing the blanket.

It was a woman he uncovered; and to see her face for the first time struck him like a revelation of horror. She had grey skin, shriveled lips, and purple beneath her eyes. He lunged back, petrified, and yelled again, and every part of him shivered, but he could not take his eyes away. He heard voices above, but they sounded distant. He drew close to the woman again as his heart pounded. The woman's eyes were closed, her hair was wiry and black, and there was a knot the size of a golf ball on her forehead.

He took more of the blanket away and something came loose upon her chest that she was holding. It was a bottle of gin. The neck of the bottle was broken off, and the cap in her lap was intact. Donny jumped backward, but his movement caused the board beneath to shift, and the bottle which was upright suddenly spilled out everywhere, and the corpse lost balance and fell to one side, nearly going off the bench, and he grabbed her by the shoulder just in the time, but the bottle came loose, striking off the bench and shattering on the walls below.

The fumes of the liquor rose. They rose with power over him, invisible and serpentine up the shaft, wafting profusely, like a prostitute's perfume. In the minute he stood in the burdened air with the grey woman, he broke into fierce, irrepressible weeping. Weeping and trembling at the bottom of the hole. He turned and stepped away, and put himself resolutely on the steps and climbed, and climbed, palm by palm, boot by boot, the voices from above babbling down words he could not understand, his helmet knocking as he went. Behind the black outline of men crouching at the top, the sky was brilliantly blue, but he did not see it. He saw one bar after the next. He could not stop weeping or trembling. At times he paused and looked at his arms while they shook, and he could not believe they were his arms.

WHAT THE MEN SAW

From the barricade, what the men saw was not something they had ever seen before. A single skull sprouting from the dark hole into the terrible, terrible sunlight, with a face streaked with weeping, the head thrown back and mouth agape, the teeth bared in a primal and inexplicable expression of sadness. And all of it drowned by the jackhammer.

There was rubble and sand on the top of Donny's head when they pulled him out and he sat there shell shocked, putting his elbow to his eyes. He whispered what he saw to the foreman, and the foreman handled the rest. He could not stop saying 'I can't help it, I just can't help it' to his men. He kept closing his eyes and sobbing into his elbow. His men drove him home, and when they arrived he sat in the front seat a moment bent forward, stricken, holding his helmet limply in his hand. He said 'I'm sorry, I'm sorry, Oh, Dad, Lord. She almost fell. She was holding it- it fell and broke." But he was speaking nonsense. He was shocked. They could see that. They told him to go inside and assured him they would take care of the rest. When he opened the door of the house his mother was standing at the end of the unlit hall looking at him.

It's just you, she said.

He didn't say anything back, nor could he. His heart was overwhelmed with what it could not say. He let out a gasp, turned his head down and went up the stairs and wept in his room. She was frightened when she saw him like that. In twenty years he never looked like that, he never had any issues with his job. She never saw him cry once.

Oh Donny. What happened? What's the matter? she said as he went up. Donny? Sweet?

She stood outside his room and knocked.

Come now, what's the matter? Let's go out and have

something to eat when you're settled. Are you hungry?

He was blubbering when she spoke, but he heard her. After a while he cried himself into a calm. He dressed and came down. Her eyes were on him, fixed, like he were someone else, and she was wearing her long brown coat, but no lipstick.

What was it? she said. I never seen you like that. Are you ok? You were early today. Earlier than usual.

He took the keys and they got in the car and drove.

You don't have something to say about this?

Not now, he said.

At dinner she kept trying to find him out, what his sobbing was for.

You can't tell me? Come on Donny. Now I feel left out. No one tells me things. What? Was it trouble? You're not getting on with those guys they assigned to you? Something. It must be. Must of been a hard day, was it? Yeah, we have those.

She took one of his hands in both of hers. Her hands were warm and soft. She looked up at him.

I can tell, she said. But I never seen you like this.

While he sat there in the booth of the restaurant he listened to her like a good son.

Yes, it was a hard day, he told her at last. He put his napkin on his plate and pushed it aside.

You didn't finish half your meal.

But she kept speaking because she suspected something else. And all her words went through him, and he loved her all the same.

The following week his tears were gone and he had come to some answer about what had happened. The men did not mention it in front of him, and he did not bring it up. They just worked hard. And later that evening, when Donny dropped them off at the pub, he came in too and had a drink. He laughed hard, and bought them drinks, and had a fine time with those men. For they were good technicians, good men, and he thought of that as he drove home late that night.

otherwise

Weeks before classes began for the fall semester, a university memo went out saying that students originally arranged to be living in the dorm hall Leviss would be indefinitely displaced to a temporary assignment in a building called Godwin. Hooper was one of them. He handed the memo to his mother who stood at the bottom of the stairs skimming and mumbling the details out loud to herself in a breathless motherly way. The old building was under sudden repair for 'water main ruptures' it said. The rest was a mystery. All that was known was that a general migration was in order. Previously assigned housing groups would remain intact; all else unchanged.

When Hooper returned to school, he arrived in front of Godwin with two large duffle bags of clothes and a backpack of books. From the outside Godwin looked more like a house than a dormitory. It had a driveway and garage on the left side that was sectioned off by orange cones, and the front of the building faced a busy boulevard. The cars that arrived to drop off students were parked end to end and had their hazards on. Hooper had never stepped foot inside the building, but he remembered it from passing it a thousand times on route to class. On the front lawn lay a wooden sign that read

'Godwin Hall - Mathematics', upturned on its back, its wet stakes exposed. It had been replaced by a plastic picket sign that said 'Welcome to Godwin'.

Inside and outside, displayed about the grounds of the building and facade were indiscriminate signs of apology from the housing department for the last minute flop. They were evidently trying to cover up Godwin's shabbiness, give it a face lift. Banners spangled the foyer with bright colors and apostrophes; there were tables with lanyards, tshirts, water bottles, laundry bags, freebies, snacks, anything to dress the old place up a bit, infect it with new life. Outside a grounds crew was hard at work mulching new plant beds, and inside the work continued; trains of last minute electricians, plumbers and inspectors of all sort went ambulating the halls, running their eyes over every last broken light fixture, clogged vent, and blotted fuse they could find. Before he moved his things in, Hooper laid his bags by the door and looked around. Godwin was smaller than Leviss by far; it was only three floors instead of ten, but where it lacked in height and large communal spaces, it made up for with a long main hall that branched off with clusters of rooms, closets, nooks and coveys, and gave it also a certain feeling of coziness. The halls were lit with candelabra that jutted from the walls, the ceilings were low, the walls snug, and the upper floors gave a bit when walked on. Between the lights, the coveys, the foot traffic, the easy carriage of noise, the lingering spirit of repurpose about the halls, Godwin was not an unpromising place to live.

Hooper received his room key from the attendant on the main floor and took his duffle bags up to the third floor. At the end of the main hallway, furthermost from the main entrance, the hall swung hard to the right revealing a secret hall, an annex with four single rooms. At the end of the annex on the left was Hooper's room, and outside his room was a large window that took in so much sun it consumed all the smaller hall lights within. There was a radiator adjacent to the window on one wall as well as a plain, white, unmarked metal box adjacent to it on the other wall.

Hooper put his bags down and lifted the top of the box to see what it was. Inside was a first aid kit, a small fire extinguisher, and a fire escape ladder, none of which looked used before. He closed the box, unlocked his room and shoved inside, the door being jammed against the frame. His room was very plain. It had a small window and a small closet. The baseboards were scuffed and the paint on the walls was unevenly colored, but overall it was fine. The light from the hallway window streamed in, making the square room a cell of brightness. It smelled of dust, disuse, graded paper, pen ink, all commingled. There were cobwebs in the top corners of the room that he wiped down with a sock. The bed and dresser were in the middle of the room mashed together. He pushed each to a corner, then swept the floor, and brought in the rest of his things and laid it on his bed and dresser. He unpacked for a while then took a break.

In the afternoon Hooper's friends arrived and he helped them move their things in. The other two were part of his housing group and were assigned the first two rooms in the annex; but it remained a puzzle whose room was the last, the one between them and Hooper. It was no one in their group. They left in the evening for dinner and afterward stayed on campus visiting other friends, then they took a drink at a bar in town, and much later returned to Godwin. When they returned to the annex the door to the vacant room was ajar, but no light was on and no sound came out of it. There was an assortment of opened boxes outside the room, and the three friends took a look inside to see what they could make out of the unknown hallmate based on the belongings they found; in one box was an electric tea kettle, in another a sleeping bag, in others pencils, pens, a trash bag of clothes, shoes, and most notably, a glass frame filled with insects.

"Well lookee here." one of the friends said. He stuck his hand in to lift the glass frame out of the box.

"We've got an odd one by the looks of this." Just then there was noise that came down the hall and he dropped it back in the box and the three of them disbanded to their separate rooms for fear they might be caught rummaging. Before bed, Hooper continued unpacking when he heard movement in the hall, loud footsteps followed by unknown voices, a woman's and a young mans, talking above a whisper. There were thuds and scrapes which sounded like they were moving something up. Hooper stepped outside to see who it was, but they were in the room already. Then the young man came out and saw Hooper standing there and said hi. He came over to introduce himself.

"I'm Ty." he said.

"I'm Hooper."

Ty was short and slender and had red hair.

"Sorry to cause so much racket-" Ty said. "We're moving things in. We won't be much longer, I think. A couple more boxes from the car."

"Not a problem. I just wanted to come out and see who it was."

"Sure, good to meet you. You don't know who else is on this hall do you?"

"Actually, the two rooms next to yours are my friends from

Leviss. We're in a housing group together."

"Oh, ok. I didn't know. I wondered." Ty said. He had an expressive face. His eyebrows twitched, he frowned, then he smiled, then he frowned, then he looked up, all in neat succession, as if each miniature expression was passing through his thoughts simultaneously. "I transferred from another school so I'm still sorting out what goes where, and where I go, and all that. You're all juniors though?

"Yes, we're juniors. And you?"

"Same," he said. "Yeah, same." Ty looked down a moment with a thought, a quizzical look.

"They may have switched a room by accident." Hooper said. "If you were planning to live with other people, or somewhere else." Then he added, "They got things mixed up with the old dorm I'm sure you know."

As he spoke he could see Ty's eyes going back and forth. It was a face full of rapt and absorbed and miniscule attentiveness, which was not pretentious, only a little odd, almost childish. Hooper noticed that the same tick, the same miniscule pulse seemed to run along the whole frame of the boy as he listened; the nodding, the blinking, a slight tapping foot- each jointed and sinewed part of the student ticked in harmony with the expression, with the face, so that listening or speaking, the whole of him showed.

"Oh, I'm not sure," he said. "I wasn't living with anyone else. Not from here. You know, I just transferred, so maybe they put me here to be with a group, or randomly."

"I don't know." Hooper said. "It could be fine. I can always ask."

"No problem though. Either way, I'm happy staying."

Ty's mother came out of the room as they were speaking

which brought their conversation to a close.

"Take good care of this one." she said, patting him on the shoulder.

She was a large and overweight woman with a rough voice, and the image of them together planted a seed of contempt in Hooper's mind. Why? He could not say. It was the way they looked perhaps; the way the mother looked especially, like white trash. They said good night and Hooper went to bed, and he was restless with the thought of Ty living beside him. The next day he mentioned it to his friends.

"You met them?" the one friend said.

"Yeah, last night they came late to unpack."

"How were they?" the one friend said.

"Not good?" the other said.

"I don't know." Hooper said. "His name's Ty. He was moving when I talked to him, his mother was helping."

"And?"

"I don't know. He said he didn't know how he got placed here. He's quirky I would say. I was going to try and talk to our RA to see if they could move him."

"It makes sense though," the other said. "Because we're in a group and it doesn't make sense that he should be there if he doesn't want to. There's plenty of other rooms. It's basically our hallway except for him."

Later that day Hooper spoke with Simon the RA who lived one floor down. Hooper explained the situation and Simon said, "I can't just remove someone you know."

"There's extra rooms aren't there?" Hooper said.

"There are, but they're in parts of the building that are being remodeled. But that's not the main issue here. The main issue is having Ty in agreement that he wants to leave. He just moved in. How can that be? You talked to him?

"Yes. It's no problem."

"When did you speak with him?"

"Last night."

"When he moved in?"

"Yes."

"You spoke to him about being relocated on the same night he arrived?"

"It wasn't me saying he should go. I just told him that the other rooms and mine were part of a housing group."

"So you suggested it?"

"He did as well, sort of. He might not want to be there either. I don't know."

Simon sighed.

"Hooper, these groups aren't meant to be exclusive. It's imperfect how it works out. Many people who wanted to live together don't get to and many who don't want to have to. The whole Leviss to Godwin move has been divisive. Plenty of situations have shifted just because of the different layout of the buildings."

"So then what?"

"So then if you feel so strongly about it either you or I could talk to him, but it needs to be very clear."

"What do you mean?"

"I need to know from him that he definitely would like to change."

"Could you?" Hooper said.

"Could I what?"

"Could you speak to him?"

"You don't want to?"

"I can, but it would seem more official coming from you."

Simon looked at Hooper and didn't say anything. Hooper made no expression; he looked appeasable and detached, like he would not be distraught or ruffled under any outcome. So finally Simon agreed, and said he would speak to him.

Hooper and his friends waited two days before they heard from Simon again. Simon called them to his room but spoke to Hooper directly when we told them he talked to Ty and that Ty preferred to stay where he was.

"He doesn't want to move?" Hooper said.

"He's fine where he is."

"He said that?"

"Yes, he said that. And he also said he never told you he wanted to leave."

"I never said he wanted to, but that he was open to it."

"Yeah, I get it, I get it." Simon said. "I know what you're saying, Hooper, but we'll leave it here for now. We're not reshuffling. There's other things to get onto. Besides, you're all in the hall together, your group. You're feet apart. Ty will be there too, ok? He is harmless. He just transferred. You could include him in things if you wanted. You don't have to, I'm not your parent. But you could. Just take care of things and it will be fine."

After that conversation the three of them dropped the subject, although it lingered on Hooper's mind, for he felt he had become the instigator of the trouble. He was the face and effigy of the misunderstanding that had aggravated from its original conversation. He resolved therefore to simply apologize, clear the confusion, and get on with other things. The next time he saw Ty was a few days later in the afternoon. Ty was entering his room when Hooper walked by him in the hall and said hello. Ty didn't see him at first and jumped at the greeting and apologized.

"Oh, hi Hooper, sorry. I didn't catch you there. Sorry, I'm easily spooked."

"That's ok." Hooper said.

Ty turned slightly. His backpack was between his feet on the ground and he stood there frozen in front of his room as if glued to the ground by Hooper's presence. His key was in the door lock and his hand was trying to shake it open. Ty was wearing spectacles that made his eyes look bulbous. He turned his head from door to Hooper, trying to talk and push himself in at the same time.

"And sorry for the- the-" but his key was jammed in the hole and he shook it till it turned and opened. Then he wedged his foot in.

"Sorry for that thing with Simon. He spoke to me. Maybe I misunderstood our first conversation. I was tired from the move, I probably misheard something. But I hope you guys don't mind if I'm here. I can stay out of your way, no problem."

"No, we don't mind. That's what I was going to say, actually, too. Sorry for that. But I don't mind. They don't either. And it's good now."

The door to Ty's room was cracked, and as Hooper spoke he glanced inside and saw the frame of bugs leaning against a bookshelf. Suddenly averting the train of his thought he said,

"Also, I noticed your little friends." He pointed. "The collection, the bugs."

Ty turned and saw them.

"Oh yeah." he said. The way he said it, it was not clear if the words were a statement of acknowledgement or a question, like he was taken aback that Hooper had seen them.

"I saw it when we moved in." Hooper said. "In one of your boxes. We were wondering whose stuff it was. You'll have to tell me more about it sometime."

"Yeah." he said. "I can do that."

"Ok good, that'd be good.

"Yeah, sure."

"Alright, I'll see you later then. And let me know if you need anything."

"I will, thanks." Ty said.

They nodded and went to their rooms. There was something stilted and manufactured about the whole exchange and the goodbye and how they parted eight feet and kept hearing each other going about their rooms and setting things down. As he lay on his bed, Hooper could hear Ty shuffling. The day was hot and Hooper began to sweat so he got up and turned his window fan on and returned to his bed and lay thirty minutes reclining wide awake, the fan purring and his thoughts wandering amiably on all the matters of his life; on class, on home, on girls, on being a junior, on intramural football; the thoughts revolved like a bright carousel of figments and faces go round, impressions of people and names, wisps of memory, gradually returning to where he was; to Godwin, to the warm room and the fan spinning and the featureless, white ceiling, and the noise from the floor below him that sounded like another technician breaking through a wall. Finally he thought of Ty, who he heard coughing in the next room. And he thought of how pleased he was by the air of diplomacy he achieved by noticing the bug frame at just the right moment - and the carousel slowed to a stop. He got up and turned the fan off and over the new silence Hooper could hear Ty talking in his room on the phone. The voice came in and out as if he were walking from one side to the next.

"They tried to kick me out," he said. Then the voice diminished and the next thing Hooper heard was,

"I'll stay right now. Yeah, yeah, I know. Yeah, it's fine. No, it's fine. I'll ignore them."

Hooper unconsciously drew close to the wall to hear those private words. His bed was against the wall of the other room and listening closer he sat down on the springs softly, because the voice was immediately next to him through the wall. He could not hear well, but what he did hear, muffled words like 'I'll ignore them' and 'They tried to kick me out' he strung together in his mind, and the more he listened the more he heard the insolence of it, and it watered the seed of contempt he had planted before. Then the speaking stopped. The room was quiet. Both were. Hooper tried getting up carefully but the bed frame budged and made a loud sound across the floor and was followed immediately by a movement in the other room. Feet hit the floor. The door flung open, then slammed, and off down the hall fled the shrew like steps going somewhere fast.

Later that evening he told his friends what he heard and the one friend shrugged and said,

"Who cares? Let him say what he says. Let him bitch."

There was a football game playing on the television in the room, and the friend whose room it was was standing, watching the game, and speaking at the same time, and when he finished his thought he walked closer to the screen and said 'Shit call, bullshit. Watch this, look here, look at this' and he waved his finger at the screen and turned the volume up and the three of them turned and watched. The other friend said 'It doesn't even matter, they're already down.'

"Shit call." the one standing said. He turned the volume down, then he sighed, then he turned the tv off for good. Then it was quiet, just the two sitting there and the one standing. The friend who was standing yawned. He sat down at the desk chair and looked at the clock.

"Let's go eat," he said. "I'm hungry."

"Now?" the other said. "Can't we wait?"

"No." the first said. "You hungry Hoop?"

"I'll go." Hooper said.

The door was partly opened and they heard footsteps in the hall and Ty's door open and close. The friend sitting on the bed said,

"There he is." and smiled at Hooper.

The other friend picked up the joke and said to Hooper,

"Looks like your buddy's here."

Hooper shook his head and said "I'm not worried about it. I'm done thinking of that. Let's go."

The friend who was sitting on the bed stood up and said,

"Keep your fan on high from now on if you don't want to hear him."

"What are you talking about?" Hooper said.

"You said you don't hear him when you run your fan, so just do that. If he keeps talking, tell Simon and he'll get moved."

"Believe me I'm not worried about it."

"Good you shouldn't be. That kid won't do anything whatsoever. He never leaves. All he'll do is talk on his phone and be in his room."

"Ok, enough. We're going." the friend said who was waiting at the door. "Are you two ready?"

"There, simple." the other friend said. He was speaking to

Hooper. Then he turned to the other friend standing in the hall and turned his voice into a whisper

"That kid's nothing. Have you seen him?"

"Shut up and let's go." that friend said.

"Seriously. I've seen him once, maybe twice." the other said as he came out. "He's dust." He rubbed his fingers together and gestured like he was blowing dust particles off the tips of his fingers. "Pure dust." Then he laughed to himself. The friend in the door shook his head.

"What? You can't handle my wisdom?"

"Yeah, let's eat, I've had enough of your shit full of wisdom." And the other was laughing and laughing.

"We're eating, we're eating. Go, move your ass."

He turned the light off and they all blundered out and the one who led the way turned the annex hall light off so it was dark and they were a bobble of shadows slinking away loudly down the hall, down the stairs and off they trumpeted, a train of foolery and shit full of wisdom going to get their bellies filled.

That night Hooper could not sleep. First he awoke to cramped legs. He sat up in the dark and tried to smooth and pound out the pain by hitting his legs with his fists but when he laid back down and tried to sleep, the cramps returned, so he decided to sit up and not do anything, until they went away. From outside the building he heard a sound like creaking metal. It was monotonous and loud, something he had not heard before. It was coming from the large hall window outside his room. He got out of bed and went to the window and looked out. High on the roof of the building was a large aluminum antenna with a dozen wiry arms, swaying and shuddering in the wind. It made a strange sound, like a moan. The back of the hall faced a pitch of woods that sloped down to a rivulet at bottom and came up the other side and opened onto athletic fields and farther on the football stadium. On game nights the lights from the stadium crept over the fringe of treetops, and down below troops of students summoned by the lights and the boombox clamor and crowd and spectacle could be seen mushing through the woods, taking shortcuts to the other side. That night there was nothing but the dark woods and the sound of the antenna. As Hooper looked out, the hallway light flicked on briefly, blindingly, and he turned around squinting to see who it was

"Who's that?" the voice said, coming down the hall. It was Ty.

"It's me."

"Oh, Hooper, it's you. You scared me. I saw someone at the window and thought it might have been an intruder. I'm not used to seeing anyone here up this late. Sorry." he said.

"It's ok." Hooper still could not see Ty until he was standing at his door. Even then he was mostly shadow and a voice. Ty was holding something in his hand.

"What's that?" Hooper said.

"This? A kettle. I had to get water on the first floor. The water up here is no good."

Ty coughed.

"You're sick?"

"I'm always sick with something. That's why I have this. If I weren't contagious I'd make you a cup but I'm not sure I am. I'll spare you for now. Next time, when we're both down, you can come by." he laughed. "Goodnight." he said. "Sorry for the light."

"Goodnight." Hooper said.

When Hooper laid back in bed the cramps were gone, but the

sound of the antenna moaned continually and now he heard coughing through the wall and then the tiny whistle of the kettle, so he turned his fan on and it drowned the noise alright and it droned all night protecting his sleep.

Godwin continued to bc gutted well into the semester until the students were blind to the presence of repair people and deaf to the racket of buzzsaws or pliers clinking through the walls. The contractors who last minute installed drywall to partition the rooms in the building had done so in a hackneyed way, leaving gaps at the bottom and top of the designated study rooms that seeped sound. Consequently most students studied elsewhere, in other dorms, in the student union, and returned to Godwin late, only to sleep and leave again by morning. Hooper amassed a pile of the repair memos and stopped reading them after a while because they generally did not affect him or the annex, for somehow the annex escaped the scrutiny of the rest of the building. The one time it was affected was for mold testing. Someone on the top floor had found mold spores, so for hours the rooms were off limits. When the floor was finally habitable again the rooms were found altered and disorderly; the mattresses overturned, the clothes thrown into closets, and the residue of a chalky pesticide like substance on the walls.

The three of them had their doors open and were putting things back in order. Ty's room was shut as usual and not a sound came from it. The two friends took a break and came over to Hooper's room and stood in the hall shooting the breeze as he reorganized. They leaned against the windowsill; one had his arms crossed and the other was looking through the metal box on the ground beside, picking through it mindlessly.

"What's in here?" he said. "Has this always been here? I've

never seen it before."

"First aid and stuff. It's been there." Hooper said.

"What for?" The friend with crossed arms said, looking down at it.

"What for?" The friend beside him looked up and said "You dumbass. Is that a question? Ask a question like that again and I'll show you what first aid is for."

Hooper said, "I saw it when I moved in. Did you see there's a ladder in there too?"

"A ladder?"

"Yeah, at the bottom. An emergency ladder for getting out the windows."

The friend with his arms crossed said,

"I suppose we could use it for our next mold evacuation. That's an emergency alright."

The one who was looking through the box shook his head.

"You're being a little shit. Maybe it was you who brought the mold for all we know." He lifted the ladder up a few rungs.

"We should use this for something though, just for the hell of it."

Hooper came out and stood in the doorway. The friend with his arms crossed turned, nudged his companion off the sill, and unlocked the window.

"What are you doing?"

"Here watch out, I want to see something." He lifted the window up and looked over the ledge.

"It's not really that high, is it?" he said. "How many feet is that? Fifteen, twenty?"

"Fifteen? Do you have eyes?"

"I've got eyes in the back of my head."

"Shut up."

"That's at least thirty. Ha, you thought each floor was five feet from floor to ceiling? You dumb shit."

"Oh shut up, before I throw you out of this."

As they were looking over the ledge a door opened and they turned to see Ty leaving his room. Ty looked at them, nodded, then walked off down the hall. Before he turned down the main hall the friend who had opened the window yelled "Hey." and Ty stopped and looked back.

"Were you the one who found the spores?" he said.

He had a mocking smile on his face. Ty did not respond; he turned the way he was going and went. When he was out of sight the other friend said "You're a little shit, you know."

"Yeah I'm a little shit, and so are you and so is Hoop. He knows I don't mean anything by it, and he doesn't care."

"There's still something about that kid that gets under my skin." he said.

"And what would that be? You've never talked to him once except for a single dumbass comment."

"Neither have you. Besides, it doesn't matter. He's got an odor. Like you said yourself, he's dust and dust gets irritable." He brought the window down and locked it.

"I just wonder what he does in that room all day." he said with his mocking smile.

"How bout you go and find out?"

"No, how bout you go and find out with him?"

"What's that mean?"

"It means what it means. You can catch a drift can't you?"

"Half the words you say mean nothing ever."

"And same for you."

"Hoop, figure this out for us."

"What?" Hooper said.

"Are you listening to this?"

"He's not listening to us."

"Who gets to go into that kid's room and find out what does all day by himself? Me or him?"

"I don't care."

"See he's not listening."

"Then we send him in first."

"Ha. Hooper, you hear that? You're taking one for the team."

"We'll give you a bodysuit for the spores."

"And the insects."

"Oh, I forgot about those. Those are in there somewhere. Yeah, and whatever other treasures he's got in there."

"Right Hoop? You hear the news?"

"What?"

"See he's not listening."

"Oh well, how did we start wasting our breath on that kid?"

"From you, you dumb shit."

And so it happened in conversations like that, which were never directly confrontational nor malicious, but offhand and unobtrusive, and tainted with the glibness that college boys possess, that the three of them went on chafing the last without his knowing. He was a mutation of their speech. The three forged an inner ring, an ironclad barrier from which to watch their last hallmate like a skirmishing spectacle, or a nonperson, to speak about him as such, and principally to keep him at a distance; out of their own affairs.

As the semester wore on Hooper and his friends spent less time in Godwin. They had class during the day and intramural football in the evenings. They played on the same team, the same team they had been on since freshman year. Besides, it was an unspoken virtue not to be a shut-in in any sense of the term; but to be out, abroad, shearing away the idle hours of college life. Godwin, by contrast, was far from the hubs of activity. And quiet. Eventually the repairs ceased and what abided the halls instead of clamors and echos was silence, a pervasive somnolence that traveled through the walls as easily as sound. On the top floor where they lived the faucets leaked in the bathroom and one could hear the leaks from the end of the hall. For all the work they put into the building there remained smells, textures, blemishes like that that could not be expurgated by any crew on a tight deadline; the smell of chalk being another one, as if years ago some unhappy student clapped blackboard erasures up the stairwells to linger forever on the air. There were the doors also, which closed some days and other days didn't, depending on the heat. They were big wooden doors and during the warm months, even into October, the wood expanded to the frame, causing them to jam. Looking at the halls straight down they made a crooked line because half the doors were flush and half the doors weren't.

On days when Ty's door was cracked, Hooper glanced into his room out of habit and saw the frame of bugs leaning on the bookshelf against a wall. It was a meager glance, and yet by it he knew everything he needed to know. He could summarize the person. The frequency with which Hooper passed the room, the crystallization of the glance, including the impression he had of Ty and the items he had seen in the boxes once, gradually construed a mental image of the space his hallmate lived in—how it was spartan, with nothing on the walls save a clock over the door; a bed, a dresser, the bookshelf, tiny piles of clothes on the ground. Tissues and kettle in odd corners, that was all.

After the few times they talked, Hooper and Ty stopped speaking to one another. The long withdrawal of words was situational more than intentional, but it produced the effect that their interactions died off, replaced by limp greetings, passing glances, perfunctory nods, and sometimes no nod at all. Completely peristaltic. If they spoke, the words were curt, general, ambivalent. Their schedules picked them up and set them down each day at separate times and separate places, rarely to cross; and if they did, Hooper had that hideous talent of naturalness. He could condescend subtly, without himself or the other knowing it was condescension. He could smile and be friendly and ask questions without inciting the slightest suspicion of insincerity. It was a collegiate virtue he had. A fluid kindness he could pour out at will. He could be all things to all people; dilating his personality for those he wished to get on with, and constricting it for those he did not. He was never malicious about it, only unconscious. There was not a bad bone in him. He was a good kid. He was tolerant and self possessed.

Hooper spent the cool Fall nights playing football on the fields beyond the woods. One evening before dusk they were late to a game and they ran from Godwin down the woods. At the bottom of the slope, they saw Ty by himself, standing off aways. He was rolling a log with his foot, and he had a plastic container in his hand. He didn't look up at their passing but kept his head down as if searching for something he dropped. Other times Hooper saw him moving from one place to the next anxiously, as if to avoid being seen or causing a stir. In the mornings Hooper would enter the bathroom while Ty was at the sink brushing his teeth. Ty would apologize, finish what he was doing, wipe his mouth on the towel, and move his things back to his room. He reminded Hooper of a krill; translucent, limpid, watery, whiskered, and the red hair of course. Even Ty's apologies were not contrite but impulsive, like a simple reflex he used to locomote, propel, disappear with.

After the football games the three friends would return to the annex and lounge in the friend's room who lived directly next to Ty. They would toss the football back and forth and eventually would hear coughing on the other side. The friend whose room it was would say to the others,

"He's always coughing. Whenever he's over there he's coughing. Do you hear it on your side, Hooper?"

"I've gotten used to it." Hooper said.

"I haven't."

The other friend said,

"Then make him stop." he said. "Give me that," He took the football, smiling, and began bouncing it off the wall.

"I'll do this until he stops."

He tossed it on the wall for five minutes straight, then the coughing stopped. Then they heard a rap of knuckles through the wall.

"Uh oh. Someone's getting tired of this sound. Now he knows what it's like to hear something nonstop."

On this went, many nights and many weeks, a series of lukewarm taunts, all of them buffered through the wall and made purely for annoyance' sake. One night they heard something crash to the ground in Ty's room.

"What was that?" the one throwing the ball said.

"Who cares?" the other said.

When Hooper stepped out to use the bathroom, Ty was in the hall trapping water coming from under his door.

"Sorry," he said, looking up to Hooper. His face was red and he shook his head. "I dropped the kettle. Everything's fine. I'll get this." He was wearing a long sleeve shirt with sleeves that came past his hands. The cuffs were stretched and squelched looking.

"You need help?" Hooper said.

"I should be fine, but thanks."

So Hooper stepped around him and left him to clean the floor alone. Back in the room, the mocking friend who enjoyed trivial displays of meddling and instigation and knavery was bouncing the ball off the wall still.

"He's not even in there." Hooper said.

"I don't care. I'll do this until he returns. Why? What happened?"

Hooper explained and the friend continued bouncing the ball off the wall, altering the trajectory so that the ball more or less brushed the wall, ticked it.

"Wonder if he'll hear this." On he went, making a rote thrumming against the wall. It was bait, solicitation, as if he hoped for some equally idiotic sound to come back; idiot morse. But it didn't come. He continued until they were all sick of him doing it and the other friend stole the ball out of the air and threw it out of the room down the hall. Days later Ty complained to Simon, and Simon met with each of the three separately and said that Ty had trouble getting to sleep because of the noise level.

"It's just a request to keep it lower." Simon said.

He gave them a sheet to sign which was a formal acknowledgement of the complaint, and they signed it. But the noise and bantering continued for weeks until the intramural football regular season ended and the playoffs began. Then it subsided altogether. After class the three friends met for dinner, then came back to the dorm, packed their cleats and left for the fields to scout the other teams and warm up. It was November by then, and the games went late. The air was brisk, the turf hard, and they played under the lights in warm black tights and blue pennies with flags about their waists. From afar, from the woods edge one could watch all the games happening at once- the fields adjacent to one another; cries, chirps of whistles, roots and cheers, all the colors of competing teams flashing in their pennies across the fields. This was college. All of college was here in microcosm; the coldness of the nights, men and women, ponytails, gloves, stretching, the undaunted profuseness of movement, onlookers, bleachers, backpacks, laughing. It was that supreme livelihood of recreation and camaraderie, convalescence, limberness, spiritedness, expenditure, ability, embodiedness; abledness. Here and now. Free.

In the round before the quarterfinals Hooper, who was one of the team's leading scorers, caught a touchdown pass that won the game and sent them on to the next round. His team hailed him at the final whistle, tackling him to the ground, and his two friends from Godwin, glutted with the victory, galloped around the field, swaggering and swinging their pennies overhead, and whipping Hooper with them. As they walked back to the dorm snow began to fall and it was everywhere in a short time, covering the fields, and everything they lay eyes on. It glistened on their eyebrows, and the woods alone were dark and untouched by whiteness. All the way to Godwin the two friends shoved their bashful champion and lauded his catch.

"I can't believe you caught that you bastard- holy shit-holy shit that wasn't real- that was insane- single handedly stripped the ball out of the other guy's grip and said 'mine, gimme, touchdown'- step aside clowns the champion's coming- the playmaker has arrived." And on they blathered him in veneration. The snow as it fell stuck on all the buildings and shimmered on the black oiled boulevard in front of Godwin before all went white, and the snow itself seemed to exalt the catch too. All night it snowed heavily and the next day classes were canceled and it kept snowing through the afternoon. When evening came the three of them had cabin fever, and they were in the room of the friend with the tv, where they had watched movies and thrown the ball around all day and were utterly restless, and were sick of it and sick of each other. The mocking friend was sitting in a chair with the clicker in his hand. Hooper was sitting on a chair beside him. The friend with the clicker yawned, turned the tv off and turned to the others and said,

"I have a headache and I'm sick of being in this shithole all day. Let's do something."

He got up and looked outside into the featureless white. The one sitting on the bed with the ball said

"What's happening out there?"

"Not a damned thing. Snow and snow. Kids stealing trays from the dining hall to sled. That's all I see."

He turned and made a face at Hooper.

"I feel like hell being in here all day."

"You want to sled?" Hooper said.

"No."

The friend with the ball said,

"We could go outside and throw this around? Play tackle in the snow."

"No." he said. "None of that. No jinxing our chances until we win that championship. These bodies are specimens."

The other laughed. "We're so full of shit. We're intramural gods."

"Exactly, I.M. gods. When we win we can do whatever the hell we want."

The friend with the ball tossed it to Hooper, and said,

"Long as this kid keeps catching."

"Yes, specially this one, our playmaker." the other said.

The friend who was looking out the window turned around with a mischievous smile.

"I know what we do," he said.

"What?"

"Come with me."

He walked in his socks and shorts into the hall to the big window by Hooper's room.

"This is what we do," he said. He opened the box with the ladder in it, and pulled it out.

"Oh, you're kidding me. Mr. specimen, let's not jinx this, my ass." the friend with the ball said. "You can eat all the words you just said."

"Let's do it."

"You can't be serious. This is about the dumbest thing I've ever seen you think of."

"Now?" Hooper said. "It's already dark."

"It won't get darker than this. You can see perfectly, all the way down the woods."

He lifted the window and the cold rushed in and snow flew in and the three of them put their heads out and looked down the side of the building.

"Look," he said. "That's not high at all. And there's bushes and snow banks directly under us - a perfect cushion. Unless you're both girls and won't do it."

He stole the ball from the other friend and threw it out the window into the snow and it hopped down the hill like a black dot and was lost in the white.

"Now who's coming?"

"You're still serious about this? How about you go down first and then we'll decide."

"I will, and it'll be fine- we've been cooped all day. Put your pants on and let's go."

He removed the rest of the ladder and threw it over the ledge, locking it on the sill, and it swayed against the building.

"What about Simon?" Hooper said.

"What about him? What's he going to do, warn us? Get us in trouble? No, nothing. He never comes down here anyway."

So they went and dressed in winter clothes and the hall filled with coldness from the open window. Beyond the window the woods had darkened; everything was a wan shade of blue and the wind blew in skeins of snow that wet the hall as it melted. When they were dressed they gathered at the windowsill.

"Now I'm going first, so you two make sure this is secure and I'll show you how it's done." The ladder clung tightly as the mocking friend straddled the sill and put his instep onto the first rung, then his hands, and took the first few lengths down as the others watched. He looked up at them as he went.

"This is what college is about boys, getting out of your comfy little rooms, breaking some rules, sucking the juice out of it." He went down a few more.

"Woo, see, perfectly fine. Not a hitch. I'm almost at the bottom."

Watching him descend soundly restored confidence in the other two to follow. Hooper yelled from above,

"Is it all you'd hoped it'd be?"

And the one at bottom said, "And more. Now shut up and get your asses down here." When he touched the ground the next friend got on. As he climbed down the friend on the ground taunted him.

"Easy does it, daisy. Nice and easy, now- don't forget your purse."

After he made it to the ground, Hooper mounted the rungs and came down.

"Let's go, Hoop!"

"Here comes our champion."

When Hooper touched ground the three of them were giddy from their descents and decided to give it one more go. They ran upstairs where the wind had picked up and the snow continued blowing slanted into Godwin through the window. The annex was colder and the floor damp and gritty from the salt they tracked in from their boots.

"Last time- here goes." the first one said.

He went down without an issue. When he touched the ground he ran and found the football and the second friend came down. When the second friend made it he ran and tackled the one with the ball, and the two of them wrestled while Hooper came down. Hooper was more than halfway down when a strong gust of wind and snow swept between him and the wall and he lost his sight. He could not wipe his eyes so he stepped blindly down cautiously, but his foot slipped on the rung, and the imbalance caused the other foot to slip off too and suddenly he hung there prostrate, dangling and yelling "Help! Help!" but the wind was howling and the wall was in front of his face. His grip weakened from the wet, cotton gloves, and as he hung there, eyes shut, feet missing the ladder, he panicked and all his yelling went silent. By the time the others saw him they were far off, muffled in snow, and Hooper when they turned fell from ten feet off the ground onto a mulberry bush beneath him that snapped on contact and he hit the ground cold, like a slab of meat.

"Hoop! they yelled, "Hoop!" but he heard nothing. His ears were ringing.

He was face down when they reached him. He was panting into the ground. His jacket was slashed open, the down running out. He groaned to his side. His bottom lip was bleeding and he held his elbow and groaned more, and the groan itself, the effort it took to make the sound was its own pain. His eyes were shut and his mouth twisted from the hurt.

"Are you ok? What happened?"

For thirty seconds they stood there looking at him cold on the ground, not touching him; shocked and useless and not knowing what to do.

"He can't move, we need to get him."

"Tell us if it hurts, we're going to lift you."

Then they stood him to his feet, one at each side. When he was upright he lurched forward, heaved, and spat blindly into the snow. His elbow and rib throbbed on the side he fell on, so he put off one helping arm and took the other. As they began to move they heard a voice from the open window, calling down the hall.

"Hello? Hello?"

The friend who held Hooper looked up and said,

"Shit, let's go!"

"Who is that?"

"It doesn't matter. Let's get him to the woods quickly before they come."

They hobbled as quick as they could and found cover behind a tree. When they were out of view they leaned Hooper with his back against the tree trunk so that he faced the empty woods. Hooper wiped his eyes with the back of his hand. He opened his eyes and they were blurry and stinging and warm. The side of his body throbbed and the taste of blood and salt was in his mouth. He raised his hand to his mouth and took off his wet glove with his teeth and laid the glove beside him on the snow and touched his lower lip with his knuckle. It was dark from blood. He leaned forward and a droplet fell from his lip. His friends were hushed. They turned facing the window, seeing who it was that called.

"Who's that?" One friend said.

"There's someone at the window."

"Simon?"

There was a pause. Hooper turned to see what they saw. He held his rib and looked up from the dark of the tree trunk and saw the figure at the window backlit against the light.

"Hello?" it called.

"It's Ty." Hooper said. "It's not Simon."

"Oh, you're ok Hooper?" the one said.

"That's good." the other said, "Ty won't care."

But they stayed there, covert and silent, watching the window. Ty looked down the hill then across the sweep of snowy woods, his eyes scanning the landscape from right to left. Between the treeline and the building the football lay in the middle of a skirmish of bookmarks where they tackled each other. Ty pulled the ladder up and closed the window and left. When he disappeared the three got up. They dusted Hooper off, gave him his glove.

"You're good." the one said. "Good as new. We'll get you cleaned off. What the hell happened? What'd you do? We looked over and you were dangling."

That friend, the mocking friend spoke with the same chummy tone he always spoke with. Hooper glared at him.

"What Hooper? What?"

"Just shut up." the other friend said. "He fell, dumb shit. You don't need to ask what happened. You saw what happened."

"Yeah, I know he fell, but how? We both got down fine."

"Just shut up for now. Get the ball."

"Fine," he said. Then he turned to Hooper and said "You'll be fine. You'll be ok. Are you going to say anything?"

"Let's go." Hooper said. That was all. He started walking back on his own, limping and holding himself.

"Look he's good, he's good. Already back on his feet, you see."

But Hooper was not listening to him or anyone anymore. He could hear his pulse in his ear drum. All movement hurt, so he stiffened himself to restrict the pain of motion. Every couple feet he felt warm blood drip from his lip onto the snow beneath him. At the front of the building he took a handful of snow from the ground, packed it and held it to his mouth and cleaned it. Then he went in, followed by the others, and trickled down feathers behind him like a shot bird. He took the elevator; the others took the stairs. Upstairs the lights were on and the doors were wide open. Muddy footprints streaked across the floor. The friends accompanied Hooper to his room and waited in the doorway looking remorseful while he unshrugged his jacket and peeled the other trappings off and sat down on the edge of his bed, flushed and pained and the drum in his ears.

"You need anything?" they said.

"No." he said.

"Ok, sorry about that, Hooper. I'm sure you'll feel better tomorrow. You can walk fine which is good. We'll see you tomorrow. Let us know. You want us to get this light?" He nodded. They turned his light off and he sat upright in the dark for minutes, hugging his side. He stuck his hand under his shirt and grazed over the ribs with his fingers; every inch stung and was sensitive to the touch. He listened to the wind outside bristle against the glass of his window, and he could hear the antenna twinging. His mind was clotted with grayness and headache and the vagrant sounds. When he had heard enough he lengthened himself on the bed, keeping himself extra still, then drew a cover up and shut his eyes for sleep.

When he woke his hand was over his side; the pain was fresh and daylight blared through the window. It was nearly noon the next day and he had overslept his only classes that day which were in the morning. Overnight the pain settled further into his bones and he struggled to dress. As he dressed himself he noticed the lifeless, sickly pale of his body in contrast with his ribs which were dark purple and the long, dried laceration marks that ran up and down his arms and legs. After he dressed he called home, and his mother told him to go to the health clinic to be checked on. When she asked what happened he said it was from football. Later that day he hobbled to the clinic and told the same thing to the nurse who saw him. When she examined his arm and asked how he got the long slashes across it, all he could proffer was that it must have happened when all the bodies were piled on him. "Your elbow is sprained and your rib is broken." she said. "The rib will take the longest to heal."

"What do I do?" Hooper said.

"Nothing." she said. "Nothing but heal. Take the prescription I give you, but other than that you need to rest. Limit your exertion; you can walk on the treadmill if you like, but no more football this season." So she sent him and he returned to Godwin with an arm sling and a bowed head and a prescription of maximum strength ibuprofen.

The recovery was slow and torturous, not least because he was pain and every move he made announced the pain, but because he was emphatically alone those days. Daytime was the loneliest time by far to be in the dorm, and the private hours he lay and sat and lay back again and looked out the window and watched the clock, produced upon his mind the vilest thoughts, mean solitudes, blunt and raving anger. He had permission for a week's leave from his classes. Some of the lectures he watched from his room, but others he skipped and had no attention for whatsoever. He also had no one to speak to. The lack of stimulation in combination with the regularity of measly cat naps he took to avoid the pain of thoughts, especially that we would not be playing in the football games ahead, made him drowsy, made him hallucinate for moments when we woke in darkness not knowing the hour and believing he heard something or someone; but listening close, hearing nothing, not the antenna, nor the kettle, nor any sound the building made, nor any voice he recognized. All he could do was listen, for hearing was the one sense that he had any kind of mobility with. The rest of him was torpor. Some days he would lie there, and the door of his room by its own accord would creak open and a rapier of light from the hall would slide along the floor onto his shoulder. His eyes would roll back to see who or what opened the door, but it was none: phantom contractions in the building. The longer he was still, bedridden, mending, the more that he was beset by inklings of an ulterior presence that he could not pinpoint. In the evenings his friends returned and checked on him and asked if they could get him anything and he said no, but they brought him food anyway and he ate it, and they talked while he ate, then threw the remains away when he was done and said bye. They had pitiful looks on their faces when they said bye, but then they returned to their room and kept talking with the tv playing in the background. He grew tired of food, of eating, of being brought meals, of the looks of guilt he received, of the material dependency on the body. What he wanted was what he had before the fall; it was something he could not name; almost a purity, an ease of being. It was something more solid than food, even more solid than health; it was real and visceral, he craved experience itself and time itself at his disposal to spend as he wanted. The next day the friends returned, and the next, but the day after that was the semi-finals, and when they came with food for Hooper they only dropped it off. They could not stay and talk.

"Gimp-" the one friend said, "You should be out there with us. You better be cheering us in spirit. We're winning this one for you."

"Go on then." Hooper said.

His friend grabbed Hooper by the leg and gave it a little shake. He was holding his cleats in his other hand with the laces knotted together.

"Yes, that's what I like to hear."

Off they went carrying their cleats, hollering down the hall and down the stairs until Hooper heard them no longer and wished bitterly he was with them, not left with the styrofoam box of food and the small square window.

Cheering in spirit meant sitting there half awake, with envy he could feel in his throat, picking at his food and picking off pieces of scab on the long cuts on his leg. He ate what they brought him, but it was too much and he felt sick from it. And he sat awake feeling that too. As nightfall came his eyes were fixed on the window. The room became hot from the heater and he sweated in his bed and the room smelled stale from loafing. The hours went slowly by. When he got up to go to the bathroom he met Ty, who was leaving the bathroom at the same time.

"Hi Hooper." Ty said. He saw Hooper in that condition. "Oh. What happened?"

"I broke a rib playing football." Hooper said.

"Sorry to hear. Is it ok?"

"I'm ok. I can't do much. It takes a while to heal, the nurse said."

"Oh, sorry," he said. "I know about that. I've broken plenty myself. Let me know if I can do anything."

"Thank you. I will."

Then they went their own ways. It had been a long time since they had spoken, and there was part of Hooper that would have liked someone to speak with, if not about something special, than anything really. To exchange words. But he did not ask.

Hooper's rib shot pulses of pain at the slightest movements awry; so did his mind, with the same sensitivity to agitation notice the slightest changes in his thoughts. His lameness did not limit his powers of inspection, it magnified them. Back in his room his mind turned over the interaction just then. It turned over Ty. As with all their previous interactions, Hooper did not know what to make of Ty, for though they were nearly always cordial to one another, Hooper's view of him was addled with disdain, or peevishness; a residual feeling of dislike that he could trace to their first conversation, that first misunderstanding. It clung to all the impressions he made of Ty afterward. If Ty was contemptible it was his slightness that was contemptible; it was the cough, the kettle, the timorous, krill-like manner; something sly, something browbeaten. The shavings of his presence. It offended something proud and collegiate in Hooper.

What more was there to know of him? The longer he stayed in bed the longer he speculated, and the more he speculated the more he laid up reserves of contempt for Ty; but it was not just Ty he had contempt for- it was for the other friends and for himself and for school and for the dark mobility of his mind which seemed never more avid and seething as when his body was feeble and inert. Hooper was alone, and at odds with himself, and his mind stirred, and the ambivalent, pointed feeling of betrayal bellowed within him, and every hour he lay by himself, *pity*, like a long black thread sewed him up in a carapace of disturbia.

What he did to free himself was get out of bed occasionally and walk to the bathroom and down the hall, and when he returned to the room he played music on the radio to break silence, and used his free arm to clean the room, establishing little amounts of order. Then rest again. Off and on, these chores. And rest was one of them. When his friends returned from the game, they were winded from victory and they came straight away to Hooper's room telling him all that happened; how another miraculous catch won the game, sending them through to the final.

"You should've been there. Ah, kills me, you should've seen

this catch- it was like yours, just like yours." The friend reached through the air, demonstrating.

"So perfect, I'm telling you- this guy takes it out of the air like it was nothing, nothing, ah, so good it hurts. Ah Hooper, Hoop, how are you doing? You should've been there. You should come to the next. We're in the finals! Can you believe that? We're bringing home the trophy like we said. So how are you doing? Sorry I keep talking, I'm just excited. You were cheering weren't you? We could feel it on the field."

"Better." Hooper said. "Very slow."

"Better, that's good to hear."

"That's amazing you're in the final." Hooper said.

"It's too good, I know, I know. I need to remind myself it's just intramurals, but I can't. The instinct takes over, the championship instinct."

The other friend lunged at him, boxing and roistering.

"I.M. gods!" the other friend said. "We're full of shit you know, Hooper. We'll leave you alone."

"Oh! We all are." the mocking friend said. "But I can't help it, we're in. We're in the finale."

"But anyway, so glad you're doing better. We'll let you rest. Ah, you needed to be there, seen this catch. You will. We'll do it again. And you'll be there next time."

"Alright." Hooper said.

The other friend scooped him away and off they went down the hall, spilling over with all their pent up excitement. Though Hooper hardly got a word in, he recovered somewhat vicariously under their harangue of high spirits, and that night he slept good, he slept soothed of the trouble of thoughts.

But by morning and the days following, the racing mind commenced and at times it got so bad it made him short of breath. He wondered if there was something the matter with him, yet aside from his thoughts he was healing slowly, gaining his step back, moving more. Whenever his friends saw him they reminded him about the final,

"We need you out there with us. No you, no us. It's going to be epic, you need to be there. Come, seriously. You're part of this team, Hooper."

"I'll try and be there." Hooper said.

"No, no, you will be there. Not if- come on, you need to. You can walk, come on. This is it."

Then the game was five days away, and for three days it snowed again, dusting everything white. During that time, all the friends spoke about was scouting reports on the opposing team.

"I've heard they're big but not quick. We have quickness. They barely beat that one team we walked over."

"They're the only team we haven't played, right?"

"Yeah, but based on who they've played, which is basically the same as us, we have the better record."

"Yeah, but championships are different."

"Not that different. If we play the way we've played all season long we take the trophy no questions about it. If we prance around like girls then we lose."

On like that it went as Hooper listened in. It was though they found the lead up, the scouting and hype-talk irresistible, almost as real and palpable as the game itself, so often they recalled it, foretold it, analyzed it, drooled over it. Hooper sat in the room appeasing them by being there, though he didn't have an opinion about the game. He knew nothing about the other team.

Two days before the game the snow turned to sleet, and the

ground grew wet, and the air became the cold that seeps into clothes. The day of, the sleet had vanished and Hooper woke to the din of rain outside plinking off the gutters. The sky was shale colored and the antenna moaned in the wind. Hooper's friends approached him that morning and said they would wait for him outside Godwin to walk over to the fields together. But when that time came, they were not there. Hooper stood at the stairs of the main entrance alone. He looked around from under the hood of his poncho, waiting. The rain was drilling and cold all day. After standing a while longer he reasoned that they had gone ahead already to prepare for the game, and so he went on his own, around the side of the building, off the concrete sidewalk, and down the muddy slope to the woods, to cut through. Sure enough, far up ahead he saw them emerging on the other side, the two of them like twins in their matching blue pennies and tights, running toward the fields. Overhead the sound of rain on the canopies of trees made a papery sound and it went whooshing along the rivulet below.

At the edge of the woods on the far side Hooper stayed and watched. He did not go farther. The dryness and the woods kept him. The pain in his rib and arm flared from the weather, the seeping coldness. And the pain kept him. He watched as his friends practiced and warmed up, appearing impervious to the coldness and wetness. There was a light fog that hung over the championship field. Music blasted from the loudspeakers and the lights were on full beam. The players darted and huddled and called through the fog; yells and whistles; streaks of flags; the haziness gave the scene a spectral mood. The daylong rain had eaten away the luster of snow, and the fields were splotched, mired dark in the places where the cleats stamped. Hooper watched his team gather at the sideline, their necks bowed together as someone from their midst roused them to a pitch of excitement, and off they ran to their starting positions.

So absorbed had Hooper become watching them he hardly moved. He was still as a post. Movement made him wince, so he channeled himself into his eyes, his thoughts. Yet, watching the players run freely, his mind, as before, filled with envy and the sublimated anger of the days of interment. He was at odds with himself; yes, it was his body, his manifest body jeering at him. Its immobility, its cumbersomeness, its lameness; the envy and the strife that were in him, rationed until then, both seized upon him, and at the whistle at the end of the first quarter, he turned back, grasped his tucked elbow, and dragged himself to Godwin. In his room he slopped the soaked poncho off on the floor and sat on his bed, trying to calm himself. His body was hunched and he drew short breaths. The rain was dancing across the window. His shoes were still on and he made no effort to remove them. The puddle from the poncho drifted along the ground toward his feet, spreading. He watched the wetness gather as if he were a frozen bystander whose sense organs - eyes, ears, skin, nose worked in strict isolation from each other. Neither was he motivated nor able to halt or stop the wetness that spread on the floor.

His body enclosed a pain that was wordless, a pain that was inseparably his thoughts, imagining the players on the field, and the bodily hurt that brooded within him like a bleak ember. The thought was the wound and the wound the thought. He tried to soothe himself by laying down, and for a moment while he laid- an eye in the storm- he heard the sound of Ty laying into the frame of his mattress through the thin walls at the same time, both beds being in the same adjacent position in the corner of the rooms. But when the quiet resumed, the mean and deprived sensations returned impassable and unbecalmed. He turned his neck from side to side, he alternated placing his arm above and below covers trying to secure some posture that would alleviate what he felt. His thoughts rambled so that he could not tell which was pain and which was the thought of pain, so entwined they were. He got up and went to the bathroom and washed his hands, and took a drink of water. On his way back to his room, Ty opened his door and looked out and said,

"Hooper, are you ok?"

"I'm ok I think. I'm just a little off."

"Ok, just checking. I heard you, that's why. Let me know if you need something."

"Sure, I will."

For a time after he laid back down the feeling settled. His mind by some involuntary reflex returned to the field where the others played and he saw them running through the haze of rain on that cleat-torn pitch, unhindered, with mud up their calves, and their eyes like marble, and the huddles they took, close and sensuous. He could almost feel their hearts racing in his own chest. How he wished on that pallid, dreary night to be out of himself, to be as the others were; vain and sleek, smoking in the dark. Under the influence of these thoughts he began counting his heart beats, one after another. His resting rate rose. The counting fed the beating and the beating sped. The more he tried to suppress the counting, the more his mind, like a rival, turned to it and counted the more. Higher the rate rose and the breathing shortened, and he began breathing louder and louder, and on it went until it triggered into a full panic attack.

It happened suddenly, the switch from tremor to panic; he

felt like he was treading death, that his body was on the verge of collapsing. His mind was somehow tripped of reality yet conscious of it too, utterly scared, like he would crumple to the floor at any moment. His breaths were spurious and swift and shallow; they came out of him as though they were being leached away, vacuumed. His lungs were in a quicksand. He stood and went desperately to the room next door and knocked. Ty opened and Hooper said,

"I need help. I need help. Can I come in?" He spoke quickly, pleading, not loud.

"Come in." Ty said. "What's wrong?"

"I don't feel right. I don't- I don't know. I'm sorry, I don't- I can't breathe. Something's not right. Something's happening."

He could not articulate what he meant with words. His blood was different.

"Here, sit here." Ty brought him to the bed to sit. Hooper saw nothing but the bed and heard the voice. His vision was spotted; his periphery was blurred, but what was close, what was immediately in front of him he saw lucidly.

"What's going on?" Ty said. He was looking at Hooper and Hooper was looking straight ahead at the floor.

"I think something's wrong."

"What do you mean?"

"Something's wrong with me. I don't know. It's my breath. Like something might happen. I'm panicking. I can't breathe."

Ty stood and brought Hooper a bottle of water.

"Here, sip this. See if this helps."

Hooper took the bottle and drank it. His eyes were watery; they were the eyes of a scared animal, open and alert and obedient.

"Try to breathe a little slower." Ty said.

"Ok I will."

Ty sat beside him watching him. Hooper could not see him but he could feel the presence beside him. He could sense the eyes on him as he tried to steer his own breath under control, bring it down, but his heart kept beating fast. Ty rose again and retrieved something from a drawer. Hooper did not look up to see what it was. He could hardly see anything but what was directly before him. Outside of him was fuzziness and inside of him was the continual quicksand sensation of wanting to collapse or faint. Ty crouched before him as he sat and said,

"Look up. I want you to look here." Hooper looked up and Ty clicked a pen light on and shined it slowly across his face, searching into his eyes. He went in one direction, then the other way across. Then he clicked it off and said,

"Your pupils look fine to me."

Ty put the light away and came back and sat down beside Hooper.

"Let me know how I can help, ok? Try to slow your breath some more."

"Ok."

"You need anything else?"

"If you just talk with me." Hooper said.

"Ok."

Hooper resumed looking at his hands in his lap, and he tried to slow his breath by focusing on it. Ty sat beside him.

"Oh, you know what?" he said. "I haven't shown you this yet have I?"

He rose again and brought the glass frame of insects from the bookshelf and laid it in Hooper's hands.

"You asked about this a long time ago. I never got to tell you about it."

"I remember this." Hooper said. As he looked it over, Ty sat next to him pointing out the various specimens, and Hooper became absorbed by it; he looked like a boy with a picture book. His heart was still beating away and his breaths were short, but his eyes were rapt, as if he were trying to anchor them on something. The insects were meticulously pinned in the case and there were labels beneath with their names. Ty went row by row, explaining the various taxonomies, but there was nothing so stunning to Hooper as the colors. All the times he had passed the room and seen the frame out of the corner of his eye, he never saw this. But here, held close, the whole pane glittered like gemstones- the pearl wings of a moth, the shiny black and emerald exoskeleton of a beetle, the amber underwing of the jewel beetle, the blue-green dragonfly, and the fruit fly whose body was the profuse colors of spilled motor oil. They were iridescent, and Hooper fanned the colors by tilting the frame to the light.

"This grasshopper I caught behind my aunt's house." Ty said. "This part is called the spiracles. Then there's the thorax, the forewing, the eyes. They have compound eyes." As they sat there they heard footsteps coming into the hall. Ty lowered his voice and took the frame from Hooper and said quietly,

"Your friends are back I think."

Hooper turned his face to the door. "I know," he said. His eyes were glazed and weary looking. He brought his finger to his lips. "I'll stay here for now." The footsteps were the only sound in the hall; no bombast of voices, just the footsteps, which told Hooper how the game ended. The shadow of feet passed Ty's door and continued on to Hooper's room. They could hear the two outside in the hall talking.

"He's not there."

"Where is he?"

"He's got to be here. His lights on, his door's open."

"Bathroom?"

"I don't know."

"What should we do?"

"It doesn't matter, we'll see him soon."

"Should I leave his things?"

"Yeah, put them on the bed."

Then they turned the other way and walked down the hall, and the shadow of feet passed under the door again.

"Let's go."

"Where do you want to go?"

"I want to get out of here. Anywhere but here. This place makes me depressed. What a shit game. There's no one here."

"What about Hooper?"

"He'll be here when we get back."

So they left and went somewhere. When they were gone, Ty handed the frame back to Hooper.

"We don't have to look at this anymore if you don't want. Only if it helps."

"It helped." Hooper said.

"How are you doing now?" Ty said.

"Better."

Very gradually Hooper's breathing had slowed and his mind too. He stopped counting heart beats. He handed the glass frame back to Ty and said, "Thank you, that's what I needed. I'm sorry for intruding, sorry for that."

"Don't be." Ty took them and put them back on the shelf. "I'm glad they were useful," he said. "I'm surprised they were. I've had them a long time. I see them so often I never think of them."

When he was stable, Hooper stood up.

"Thank you again, Ty. I don't know what happened. That had never happened before. I'm sorry for bothering."

"Sure Hooper, it's no problem. It wasn't a bother. If it happens again let me know."

Ty opened the door and Hooper stepped out.

"I guess I'll see you around then." Hooper said.

"Yes, sounds good."

"Thank you again."

"No problem." Then they parted.

The hallway smelled of snow and wet wool and body odor. Clumps of turf littered the hallway and the two pairs of rotten cleats were lined against the wall. On Hooper's bed was a trophy; with a chrome gold figurine of a football player and a plaque across the front that read - Intramural Football, Runner Up. The whole season, and maybe the whole semester, and maybe much more was summarized by that trophy, and there was something implacable in Hooper; a frigid and irreverent pleasure he had knowing the game went the way it did, having been elsewhere and otherwise: and not for worse. When his friends returned they were crestfall and low. They gathered in the room with the tv, and the one friend threw the ball against the wall as was his habit. Hooper asked what happened and he said 'You saw the trophy didn't you? We got trounced'. The friend who was sitting said, "I'll give them they outplayed us, but we were missing people. Imagine if we had this fool.' nodding at Hooper. 'Plus the refs were terrible, absolutely awful. Blind as moles. If we had other refs, different story, different outcome. Next time, Hooper, you'll bring it home for us. We could've won though. If everyone was there, we could've. We were missing players, and the refs I mentioned, but still. They were crooks."

Hooper and the other friend said nothing. The one kept throwing the ball against the wall, and for a while that was the only sound there was.

Weeks later winter break commenced and Hooper returned home and rested until he was healed and back to normal. His sling came off and the bruises disappeared. At times during the langor of the day he recalled the evening of the panic attack, but he told no one of it. His mother asked how school was and he said 'fine'. And she said 'what about your friends, your two friends? I can never remember their names. You've mentioned them before but I can never tell them apart.' And he said they're fine too.

When they returned from break Ty's room was empty. Simon informed them that Ty moved down a floor by request. Classes began and some afternoons Hooper stopped in the stairwell on the second floor and looked down the hall where Ty's new room was. It was at the very end. An exit sign dropped from the ceiling and it glowed from afar like a red pin of light. Upstairs the friends convened. The doors were flung open and they floated about the hall freely and loudly, for it was all their own. In the odd room light patched the floor through the small, square window, and no one went in there but Hooper. In secret he stored his fan and trophy in the empty closet, and in the dark they remained there, gathering dust.

Strongman

For three days in July a traveling carnival descended on the small town of Glen Burnie, Maryland, hammering stakes and pitching tents over the large fairground field beside the fire station. The field was yellow and trampled, worn from overuse and far from being fair in any sense of the word. The locals knew it better as the 'dumpgrounds'. Most of the year it staged junk car auctions and drew lowlife from nearby towns who swarmed the place in tattoos and wife beaters, belched the air with loud, fatuous mufflers, and littered the ground with chicken bones, energy drinks, and pornos.

The proprietor of the auction was a man named Wilson Wingate, a gaunt, fast-talking geezer who was known in town as a charlatan and hustler. Beside the auctions he owned a dollar store called the 'Trot Stop'. On the sign of the store was a turkey, out of whose beak blurted the tagline 'Gobble up the savings!' Wilson was a skinny man who had long grey hair and wore brown suits with American flags pinned to the lapel. Years ago a stroke paralyzed half his face, so when he spoke half his lip curled and half his brow furrowed, giving him a permanent sneer. But however ugly it was to see him talk, one could not help pay attention to the talking itself, for out of his skinny body came a foghorn of a voice; a voice made for radio, for announcements. It was theatrical and seductive, a sound people could not help listen to. A sound made to be heard.

Every year the carnival recruited local hands, and every year Wilson Wingate volunteered to man a booth, or tear tickets, or operate a ride. He went wherever they put him. The whole town chipped in, including Mart Peterson's family. Mart was the deputy of the fire department which owned the fairgrounds and monitored the carnival during its days in operation. He had known Wilson for years, and the two of them had a wary relationship. After every car auction Wilson approached the fire station with a soiled wad of bills and licked his thumb and counted off a thousand dollars damage for renting the fairgrounds and cleanup fees. He gave it to Mart saying,

Alright here Marty, here's your lunch money. Now don't you and the boys go spending it all on pretty girls.

Then he slumped off and Mart watched him narrowly, suspicious of where he might go or what he might do next. He warned his children of Wilson for he knew him to be cunning, and he did not want them tangled in his affairs. Mart's son was named Mitch, and his daughter was named Madison. They were twins, both seniors in high school. They were tall with brown hair. Mitch was a football player, Madison a basketball player. Every year they helped set up for the carnival, and that year Madison was chosen by her high school to be 'Queen of the Carnival'. Mart's wife, Samantha, was homebound, and every year she told her kids to win her a prize and come back and tell her all about it. And every year they had.

Like his father, Mitch was distrusting of Wilson because of a car he sold him at auction two years ago. It was his first car, a jalopy Thunderbird that began breaking down the moment it left the lot, and was beset by repairs as long as he owned it.

Mitch bought the car against his father's warning and spent his entire savings on it. Weeks after he bought it he called Wilson for a refund and all Wilson said was, Buyer assumes risk. I can't offer any recompense. Then he hung up the phone. Angry and determined to get his money back, Mitch drove the car down to the auction office at the fairground. The office was a trailer house with a dirt lot outside. It was midday. The lot was empty and all the blinds were down. Mitch parked in the dust and revved the Thunderbird loud for five seconds before it sputtered and made a sound like a stick being jammed into bicycle spokes. It was an ugly sound and he wanted Wilson to hear it through the paper walls of the office. Without knocking he came in. Wilson was at the far end of the trailer, sitting behind a desk with his feet kicked up. Mitch walked toward him and Wilson said,

I hear it alright. Makes me want to put a screwdriver in my ear.

He laughed and took up the green jar of pickles on his desk and leaned back in his chair. The lid popped and he stuck a toothpick into the briny green water and drew one out and slurped it.

Fresh one, he said.

He leaned forward and offered the jar to Mitch, who did not take. Then Wilson leaned back, put the jar on the table and fished another slice of pickle and slurped it.

That must be your car out there disturbing the peace.

He wiped his mouth on his sleeve and adjusted the brim of his hat. It was a suede brown hat with a wide brim, and he wore it tilted up.

It is, and I'd like a refund, Mitch said. I just bought this car days ago at the auction and it's already doing this. It overheated twice. The first night I brought it back it overheated. I barely got home.

So what are you saying?

You sold me something broke, he said.

I sold you nothing of the sort. I sold you a fine car, as far as I'm concerned. You drove it around before you bought it, didn't you?

Just around the fairground.

Well then, that's on you, not me. That was your judgment. And I'm sorry, but I can't do nothing about that. Buyer's responsible after it leaves the lot. I can't tell if a car's gonna snap as soon as it leaves the lot. God knows that. I run a business with things that break. And that's how it's always been. And that's the way it goes.

Wilson swiveled in his chair and pried his finger through the metal blinds and looked outside at the car.

Yeah, he said. No way to tell on these sorts of things. No way. Wish there were.

He sighed and swung around.

Damn it's hot out there, he said.

He kicked his legs up on the desk again and leaned back with his hands folded on his belly. He blew out of his teeth a slight whistle.

Now what? he said.

I can't drive it. Mitch said.

You drove it here, didn't you?

I did but-

But no! he said. He raised his finger in the air and smiled. You see? You did drive it here, so you need to try and be accurate with your assessment of this ve-hicle. It runs as far as I can see.

It was only a ten minute drive.

Nonetheless, nonetheless.

Mitch was furious in his mind, but he saw there was no moving the man. He put his hands in his pockets and felt the keys at the bottom, warm and greasy.

What can I do if I can't get a refund? he said. That was my savings.

You drive it back where it came from, or, I'm happy to tow it for free if you leave right there. But that's all.

That's all?

Yes sir, that's all.

Mitch shook his head.

Take or leave? he said.

I'll take it, Mitch said.

Then he turned around and walked slowly out, his large footsteps creaking over the flimsy floor. He opened the door up the front and turned once more to Wilson and glared, but Wilson did not see him. His jar was propped on his belly and he was fidgeting with the cap. Mitch drove home and left the car to waste. To soften the blow, his father took it around to repair shops to see what could be done, but every estimate was twice the cost Mitch paid for it, and in the end they gave it up. For months it moldered at the end of their driveway until they donated it, but ever after Mitch remained jaded by the transaction, and everytime he saw Wilson he saw the likeness of the Thunderbird spewing smoke out of the hood and having to be yanked off the road and whistled for help.

A week before the opening, Mart and Mitch helped build the booths and string lights around the outside of the fairground. They laid hay for the petting zoo and helped build a cage for the newest attraction that year, a great, full-maned lion named

Charlie. In broad daylight, before the tents were raised or the rides running, when the yellow earth lay covered in a heap of metalwork, canvas, and cardboard boxes of cooking oil- it all looked so flat and unimpressive. But it is amazing what night does. On opening night when the neons were lit, the colors streaming, the fryers sizzling, laughter peeling abroad, tickets ripping, and the far off beating of drums. All the stirrings and clamor. The carnival woke. It had a primal power over the imagination.

Mitch came the first night with his girlfriend, Claire. From afar they saw the two revolving lights shooting up into the night sky, and as they got closer the fairgrounds thickened with crowds, and the sound of games and whirling rides thrilled them with excitement. Inside, they strolled slowly, lost in time. They turned their heads from sideshow to sideshow, imbibing the various games and diversions; the ring toss, the fortune teller behind a velvet curtain, the fun house, the tilt a whirl. Smells of muddy earth and funnel cakes and summer air filled their noses. Onward it stretched. Around bends were beer gardens and cotton candy stands and frozen lemonade carts. In the food tent people sat at long picnic tables and ate fried fare off white paper plates. Country music blasted and high powered fans threw the air around.

One emerged from every tent and heard the hydraulic hiss of roller coasters, arcade sounds, and the crescendo of screams coming from all corners. The largest and loudest ride was a pirate ship that swung back and forth, rocking higher and higher until it spun all the way around. From the ground, Mitch and Claire watched as the ship turned upside down, and they could hear coins and jewelry falling from pockets and necks into the metalwork below. Afterwards they visited the lion.

STRONGMAN

The lion tent was crowded. There were murmurs and shuffling, with everyone trying to squeeze as close to the bars as possible. They all hoped the lion would be as people imagine lions to be: terrifying and roaring and lashing at the bars and clawing bloody meat. But it was the sleepiest of all the attractions. When it woke, it stared lazily at the crowds and did nothing else but flick its tail, and loaf, and furl its big red tongue when it yawned.

People came and went. From ground level Mitch saw his father and other firemen sitting on the balcony of the firestation drinking beers, watching the carnival, and looking like they were having as much fun as the crowds below. Mitch and his girlfriend started in one corner of the carnival and walked along the border. They passed dozens of games and amusements, but did not play any because there was one game Mitch was holding out for. As they turned the second corner past the lion tent he finally saw it, standing in the very back corner. It was the hammer game. Officially it was called The Strongman. It was a tower with a bell on top, and you swung the hammer so that the needle reached the top and rang the bell to win a prize. He had won the game every year since he was in high school, and every year he looked forward to it. However, as they approached the game Mitch grew stiff and quiet and his countenance fell.

What is it? Claire said. You got quiet all the sudden.

Mitch pointed ahead.

Look, he said. Look who it is.

To his shock and disappointment, the one who stood beside the game as its operator was none other than Wilson Wingate, the man he wished most to avoid.

Wilson's running it, he said.

What's that got to do with the game? You'll be fine. Shrug

him off, Claire said. Besides, you always take something home.

I know, but I don't like him is all. I've seen him here before. He's shifty. He manipulates. I told you about the car didn't I?

Mitch knew from carnivals past that Wilson did not merely operate games, he embellished them, dramatized them. In a way, he became them. That night he took the mallet, the needle, the notches, the bell, the tall, bronze tower, the rule of three swings, and mutated them into something of his own personality. Already they could hear him from far away. The mud earth was his podium, and from it his voice boomed; coarse and strident. He dallied with passersby to lure them into the game. Claire linked her through Mitch's and she stopped him a moment as they walked and said,

Hey relax. You haven't even swung yet and you're tight. Just have fun and don't focus on Wilson. Forget about him. All he does is talk. You know that. Let him have his moment. You swing, she said. That's all you do. Just swing.

It wasn't so simple as that, Mitch thought. Wilson had whipped his pride before, and the thought of being brought to stand at the foot of the tower to become some public display of ridicule made him nervous and quiet. However he tried to focus on just the game, he could not. Not when he saw Wilson dancing around it and heard his voice trumpeting. He could not separate the game and the game lord. Yet he went on, for he knew he had won the game before, many times. The very same game. That thought alone assured him. It lowered his resistance and she pulled him along.

They came close, pushing through the crowd. Wilson walked on stilts and he was dressed in the full regalia of his showmanship. He wore a black top hat and a long red and black striped frock that swished as he moved. His pants were gold sequin and they shimmered as he hobbled from side to side, crooking his finger, leering and smiling over the heads beneath him. He looked like a cross between a crab and a scarecrow. The costume he wore was buffoonish and draping; under it he looked gaunt as ever, like he was made of wire hanger. He was unsteady on his stilts, and the way he crept about on them made him look predatory. He was stooped by age, but still almost as tall as the game. Mitch watched as people came and went, and he watched as Wilson's expression changed for as many people made eyes with him; to one he grinned, to another he winked, to another he pouted, and so on. There were a hundred subtle looks he produced with half his face. Some people turned their heads at him in fascination, others stopped and listened as he spoke, but no one attempted his game until Mitch came. Claire pushed him through, and he emerged from the crowd silent and nervous and confident. He was the tallest in the crowd, a head above the others.

When Wilson saw him he turned and came over and let out a yell of delight. He held a large red microphone that dragged a long wire connected to an amplifier below his table. The amp had a glaring red light that meant it was on. Above the table was the prize wall, on which five large stuffed bears and a dozen small animals hung from their backs. When he saw Mitch approach his eyes widened and his mouth spread wide into a grin. Ho ho ho! he said. He tapped the top of his microphone and jerked the cord free and waved Mitch over.

Marty's boy. Yes, come! come! I see you there, come. Don't be shy. My goodness folks, he's almost as tall as me and I've got stilts. This ain't fair folks! You've grown an inch haven't you. My ok, folks gather, please gather round. We have a real contender here. Your name son?

Mitch, he said.

Mitch, then. Mitch, folks. You hear? A local contender. A fine young gentleman. Look here at this well built young man. Surely we have a prize winner before us.

He turned from the crowd to Mitch and put his arm on Mitch's shoulder.

Now Mitch, have you ever played this game before?

Yes.

Well good, good. But have you ever won before?

Yes.

Yes? Well, my, what am I doing all the introductions for, we have a seasoned winner on our hands, a man with few words, and we won't let nothing get in his way now will we?

He stood beside Mitch with his arm around his shoulder and looked out to the crowd, then he turned the young man to face the game.

Now folks can we make some room for him? Clear some space. A little more. We've closed him in here. The man with the mallet is determined and we're soon to see if he's what... what do we call this game? A simple test of skill and strength, and what do we call it? Come, anyone. Spit it out!

He cupped his ear and leaned toward the crowd.

What do you say? That's right, that's right! The straaawwwng man game. And a strawnmang's what we want.

He came back to Mitch and put his hand out, the one holding the microphone.

You have to pay up first, he said.

Mitch handed him five dollars and Wilson snatched it and put it in his frock. Then Mitch took the mallet from the ground and planting his feet over the base of the tower, he spread his grip, raised the hammer high over his head and came down, sledging it as hard as he could. Wilson aped the motion from behind, using his microphone as a mallet. The needle climbed halfway up the scale on the first swing, and fell clink clink clink, back to the base.

That's one! Wilson said. Two more, let's go now.

He held his fingers up high in the air so all who passed could see. Mitch looked at the top of the tower. He couldn't believe it only went that high the first time. Then he swung again and this time the needle went three quarters to the top, just a few notches above the first.

That's two! Two strikes! Only one left. Oh, come on now, you've got more than that don't you, Marty's boy? Folks he needs some cheering, some energy, come make some noise.

On the third swing Mitch put all his strength into it and came down breathing hard like a bull. He watched the needle jump all the way to the top but fall right before it hit the bell.

Tha-ree!! Wilson yelped. That's three for our contender. One! Two! Tha-ree! You're out.

He punched the air like an umpire. Then he came over and patted Mitch on the shoulder, but Mitch shrugged him off.

You did something to that game, Mitch said. I've hit that bell before. You did something to it.

Wilson ushered him out of the crowd as he spoke.

So close, so very close. Next time, Wilson said. He pushed him along.

Same game it's always been, bud. Next time you'll get it. Come find me. Next time, don't be shy. You come back and give it another try. Now who's next? Here, yes sir. Is that you? Step right up.

Mitch looked over his shoulder as Claire pulled him out of the crowd and the people began forming a semicircle around a new contestant.

Come on, she said. Let's go. Enough with it. There's more to see.

But Mitch kept looking back, looking over his shoulder at the game and Wilson. He wore a scold on his face and he shook his head.

Did you see that? Mitch said. He's done something to that game, I'm telling you. I've beat it every year the past three years. On my first swing. That's the only game I ever won except this year.

Let it go, she said. It's a game.

Yeah, I know. But still. I hate to see him next to it. And he's rigged it on top of that I'm pretty sure.

Let it go. You can play it again another night, she said.

Maybe, he said. But his voice was half hearted.

You should. I bet you'd get it next time. You'll strike the bell, you watch. You'll make it sing.

Mitch lost his spirit for the carnival after that. They walked around a while more, but Wilson's game hounded him in his thoughts and he was disturbed by it, though he did not mention it anymore to his girlfriend. It continued eating at him that night, even after he took Claire home, and the whole next day too. He was angry at being handled by a cheat, and his anger was muddled with the embarrassment that he would take a carnival game so seriously. There was also shame in his mind. Ashamed to lose that game on three tires. And finally there was fear. Fear that the power was gone out of him, that he had actually lost strength.

Still he wanted to try again. He wanted to make the bell sing.

So on the third and final night he decided to come back to redeem himself. He came with his sister Madison who was the 'Queen of the Carnival'. She wore a sash and crown and a pearl-blue dress, and was driven around on a golf cart float festooned with streamers and beads. There were buckets of flowers and ribbons on the backseat which she handed out as she went around. Mitch was alone; but from the moment they arrived his eyes gravitated to the back corner where he could see Wilson traipsing, reeling people in. He did not go straight to the game at first. He waited before he went there. He entered tents and came out, he ate and sat down, but everywhere he walked, from all alleys and purviews, he saw Wilson out of the corner of his eye, like the axle to which all spokes joined. There he was; ruffed and alluring; the red microphone, the swinging cord. He was grand as a false prophet. To Mitch he was the epicenter of the carnival.

Finally Mitch came to the game again. He was taken into the crowd with the same loud enthusiasm as before, and when he emerged in the clearing, Wilson turned on his stilts and smiled at him darkly.

Now yes sir! Come right this way. Goody, I like this already. Folks, here we have a man in search of redemption. He tried two nights ago and fell just short. Now he's back. He has purpose, he has determination, you can see it in his eyes. But the question is: is that enough? And that's not all. Can he redeem himself with only one swing tonight?

Mitch looked up at him, suddenly confused.

What do you mean one swing? It's three swings.

Wilson laughed into the microphone, then he looked down at Mitch.

I wish it were, but you only get one swing tonight. One

swing's all you got.

He yanked the word away from his feet.

Same price.

It's always three, Mitch said. Why'd you change it?

Mitch felt his cheeks reddening before the crowd.

Not tonight, Wilson said.

Why only one?

Demand is high on the final night. You see the crowds. Look at em. Come on now.

He spun Mitch around.

Now let's go and get set if you're going. Besides, I've had too many winners. Too many strongmen. I couldn't count 'em'. We're going to be out of bears at this rate. They've been going like hot cakes. Now come step up. Folks here we go.

He was not looking at Mitch any more. He was looking at the crowd.

As Wilson said these things he glanced and saw the young man's countenance fall, and he enjoyed the response; it was his savor and relish to reduce to frustration the willing contestant. To provoke him to bitterness; to rankle a dog til it bit. Wilson handed Mitch the mallet and Mitch held it unsurely, looking evilly over at the man. At the base of the game he planted his feet and spread his grip.

Payup first, don't you forget.

Mitch reached in his pocket and gave him five dollars without looking him in the eye. His eyes were narrowed on the very center of the contact point and his mind visualized the single swing. Wilson stood behind him aping him as before. As Mitch rose the mallet high in the air, Wilson's arm went up with his red microphone. But at the very top of the motion, Mitch halted. His grip loosened and he shook his head and lowered the mallet, leaving it on the ground.

Oh, what's this now? Backing out are we? Wilson said. So soon? What's this?

Mitched stepped away and said,

I'll take my money back.

He held his hand out.

No siree, Wilson said. Once you paid, you paid. That's it.

I didn't swing. I paid for a single swing.

Doesn't matter. Wilson said. You don't have to swing. You can swing now, or later, or never, but you can't get your money back. This isn't no department store, there's no refunds here, and he laughed into the microphone, to rouse the crowd. Then he stepped aside and Mitch lowered his hand.

Now come folks, let's help this fellow off so we can have our next contestant.

He looked back at Mitch.

Sorry, he said. Swing's here if you want it.

Mitch turned without another word and kept his head down. The crowd was staring at him, and as he passed through their midst, Wilson grabbed him by the sleeve and said,

Here, why don't you take a little bear, take it for someone special, huh? Just to say you came and showed up.

He waved a small bear at him. Huh? he said.

No thanks, Mitch said. He left through the crowd and Wilson called after him.

Come back, he said, come claim your prize. Don't be ashamed. Next year, Marty's boy, next year. Next year you come back, you have better luck. You might get one of them bears for the big boys.

As Mitch walked away he could hear Wilson taunting him.

Oh, boo. You see that folks? That's called a sore loser, a poor sport. It's a hometown carnival for crying out loud. Who gives up before he even tries? Now that's not strong is it? That's weak. And we don't want weak now do we? Because what's the game we're playing?

He cupped his ear again, leaned to the crowd, then tilted his head up and roared into the scratching microphone,

We want a straaaaaaaaawnnngg man!!

Next, next, next, who's next!

When Mitch escaped the range of Wilson's bombast, he walked around for an hour searching for anyone who carried a large prize bear from Wilson's game, but he saw no one. He was glad he did not swing. It was all a ruse. To put his mind off Wilson he went to visit his father at the firestation. However, almost as soon as he arrived, the firefighters received a call from below saying there was a fire in the kitchen. By the time they got down it had spread to the food tent and people were screaming and fleeing, and smoke was coming out. Then something else happened. The tilt-a-whirl jammed and riders were stumbling off, shaken and whip-lashed. At the same time news spread that animals got loose from the petting zoo. Volunteers were scrambling. There were pigs darting between legs. The chickens vanished altogether.

Minutes later one of the high revolving lights burned out. And in the middle of the fairground, a sound like a gunshot went off, which doubled the panic. It was part of a chain of disruptions that happened suddenly and simultaneously, with no conspicuous cause except that the grounds were overcrowded. Soon there were screams and sirens and flocks of little girls running hand in hand to the nearest exit. Half the crowd bolted for the doors, while the other half turned about incredulously, not knowing what to do. Hysteria and pandemonium stretched over the fairgrounds, and no one saw Wilson Wingate standing in the middle of the chaos with a look of absolute serenity on his face. He turned side to side, looking on the upheaval with a kind of admiration. Mitch looked for his sister but he could not find her. In the haste, she had come off her float and was looking around, and she was the only one who saw Wilson standing there. She watched what he did. She saw him detach his stilts, and she continued watching him as he walked to the main ticket booth, dissembling into the throngs, pretending to escort people and direct the crowds to the exit. Under this disguise she saw him reach behind the counter of the booth, open the cash box and stuff all the bills in his coat. It was very sly and very quick, but she saw it clearly. Then he continued directing the people and escorting them, saying

This way, this way folks, keep calm folks, everything's alright. We've got good firefighters here. Everything's in order. Come now, come now.

In the crowdedness, he did not see the girl watching him, nor did he know who she was. Gradually and slyly he stepped away from the onrushers and returned in the direction of his game. She kept her eyes on him. She peered behind the corner of a cotton candy stand as he transferred the bills from his coat to his top hat. The back corner of the carnival was dark and vacant. He was by himself, and when he believed himself to be unseen, he clipped the remaining stuffed bears from the prize wall, noosed them together and slung them over his shoulder. Even when he was alone he made noise, for she could hear him whistling to himself. He went straight back behind the fairgrounds where trailers and RVs and rental equipment trucks were parked. He walked slowly. He didn't rush.

Madison walked after him a few paces, and she was nervous following because it was quiet and it was just him. She could not move fast in her dress, and her heels sank to the mud the quicker she walked. Finally she stopped and shouted his name. He did not turn the first time. She shouted again and the second time he stopped, looked over his shoulder. He was glowering and smiling at her, but she saw nothing. There was only darkness and voice where his face was.

You best turn around, he said, low and relaxed. You're only going to ruin your pretty dress.

I saw what you did, she yelled. I'll call someone, she said.

I'm not sure what you mean, honey.

Give the money back. You stole it. You took it from the booth.

I have no money but my own hard earned keep. And my shifts over. I believe you should turn the other way now.

He turned and kept walking, and he did not walk fast. Flustered and unable to stop him, Madison went back as fast she could and searched for her brother in the remaining crowd. She found Mitch by the food tent pulling tables and chairs out where the fire had been. The fire was extinguished and the tent smelled of charred wood and burned plastic. She told him what happened and where Wilson went, and after pausing a moment he told her to stay there while he went after him.

What will you do? she said. But he did not say. Nor could he, because he was afoot already, and deaf to his anger. He did not know what he would do. He walked briskly. All he knew was that he was on his way to stop Wilson, to confront the man. Before he left the fairgrounds he stopped at the strongman game. The glaring red light of the amp was still on and the microphone dropped on the ground beside it. The stilts were lying on the table. On the backside of the tower, Mitch found a rock the size of a fist duck-taped to the needle. That's how Wilson rigged it. He ripped the rock off and carried it as he left the fairgrounds and stalked Wilson from a distance.

Wilson had not made it far yet. He moved sluggardly under the weight of bears, like a tramp carrying another tramp's dead body over his shoulder. The farther back he went the quieter and darker it got. Mitched tucked behind trailers to avoid being seen. He stepped softly over the packed dirt to avoid being heard. Behind them the carnival made a bright halo of light that shrunk the farther they moved away from it. Wilson's pants were rolled up the cuff and they still shimmered in the dark. At last they came to a minivan with a wood panel stripe across its side and tinted windows. It was Wilson's van. When he reached it he dropped the stuffed animals on the ground and said without turning around,

You think I haven't heard your clumsy steps following me?

Mitch stopped in his tracks. Then Wilson turned around, his face shadowed under the rim of the hat. The ground between them was dusty yellow mud. Wilson held the bears by a length of string wrapped around his knuckles.

Why'd you follow me this way?

Mitch stared at him, not saying anything, for he was afraid and furious beyond words.

Are you gonna speak for yourself or what? You look angry. I wish I had a mirror for you to see yourself. I admire you coming all this way after an old man to tell him something. With that mean look on your face. You must be burning in your temples with something to say.

You're a cheat.

Am I now?

Wilson dropped his head, listening. He smoothed his hand down his frock. Then he looked up, sneering and Mitch could see the sneer even in the dark, even under the hat rim.

If that's the first thing you say to me man to man, I suggest you keep your mouth shut from here on, you hear? And secondly, don't use my name. Don't you dare profane it with comments like that. You don't know me. You don't know a damned thing about me. The way you followed me like a creep proves you're too coward to approach me in the open. You've grown up on the wrong side of life, and you're not twenty years old. But I won't blame you. I blame whoever raised you. So if you know what's better for you, turn right around and leave, and take your furies and frustrations elsewhere.

Mitch felt the rock in his hand and clenched it. Wilson turned to open his car and Mitch tossed the rock at his feet. Wilson looked down and saw it and laughed low to himself.

What? You think that's cheating. Oh boy you've got some things to learn. Is that why you came all this way? To rebuke an old man you don't know and tell him he was cheating. That's not cheating. That's not a mile from cheating. That's gaming. And everyone who's ever been to a carnival knows what a game is, and how they rig em'. That's the definition of a carnival game, lest you never figured that out. People don't come to carnivals to win prizes. They come to piddle around for a while, to get lost. Losing's not the worst thing to happen at a carnival. It's respectable, long as you try. Is that why you came?

He nudged the stone with his foot. No? Then get out of here.

That's not why I came, Mitch said. You stole money from the ticket booth.

Did I? And how would you know that?

Someone saw you.

Someone saw me.

He laughed low to himself again. He opened his frock and took the pockets out one by one, patting himself down. Each pocket he pulled had a silk lining to it, and he left it that way.

You're watching, aren't you? If you can tell me where it'd be I'm happy to turn in. You want to come over here and search me yourself? You must have got the wrong guy, he said.

It's not there. It's your hat.

My hat? Well, that would be nifty now wouldn't it?

He took off his top hat and threw it to Mitch like a frisbee.

Go on then, find my spoils, tell me what you find.

Mitched searched the hat inside out. It was a trick hat with a secret flap compartment in it, but there was nothing inside. Wilson wiped his bald scalp with his hand then wiped it on his leg.

Now are we done here?

My sister saw you.

Your sister. Your sister, who? She saw me where? Oh, yes, he said, the remembrance coming to him. Oh that was her calling after me. Uh huh. I guess she saw me with those pretty eyes of hers. Well then. Well how bout you get back and tell her what you found on old Wilson. I'd tell you to call the police, but I don't know what you'd tell them when they got here.

In the distance a car alarm went off. It squwaked and made a pale orange pulse off Wilson's face.

Again you don't have much to say do you?

He jigged the rope in his hand and the bears shook.

Tell you what. You came all this way, why don't I give you one of these here bears, and we both forget you came here on a fool's errand, to prove something you can't even spell out. You take this prize, and you tell your folks you won a prize tonight. Give it to your sister. Better yet, give it to your mother. She could use one, couldn't she?

Mitch stepped forward, his hands clenched at his side.

Don't speak about either of them, he said through his teeth.

Fair, but I suggest you do not step one foot further.

Wilson pulled a small pistol from his frock, the same kind of gun that fired into the air and caused a panic.

Because then we'd really have some trouble. You're too good of a kid. You're Mart's son I know. Spitting image of him too. Is that why you really came? To prove something to him? You've said all your words I know. But let me tell you something. Then I'll be going.

He lowered his voice and leaned back against his van.

You need to learn to speak. Ones like you are too afraid of saying a wrong word. That bottled anger. You need to learn how to put someone on their back heels. Learn to speak. Find some devil in you. You're too nice, you're like your daddy. You want to know about your father? I'll give it to him, he's a fine man. But don't think he's spotless. He's embroiled himself in his own trouble. Every time I run my auctions, afterwards I walk over to him and pay out 2,000 dollars of my own hard earned living so he'll keep his mouth shut about the activities people get into on that damned fairground. He tells the station it's all rental and cleaning fees right? No, no, no. They right well know what we're up to. Not me, but my customers, my patrons. It's good ol' extortion, and he's more than happy to take it because he's looking out for that raggedy fire department. They're poor as bones. They need benefactors like me. He doesn't tell you that now does he? You see you must speak. And he doesn't speak the same as you. Silent ones like you sit in the squalor of their thoughts, thinking all the same exact thoughts but having no guts to speak it. I think that's cowardly. They're afraid. They've no strength or compunction to speak their minds. But enough of my sermon. Listen, you come work for me at the auction and I'll teach you. And I'll get you something better than that lemon you drove around for a while. The one that squealed up to stop lights.

He laughed to himself and tilted the gun up.

I've made my living from this hole in my face, and I believe that's something you can learn from.

He did not raise his voice when he spoke. His words flowed together almost elegantly when they were not strained, yet even then they were not truly elegant words but ugly because they were lies. They were dry and rustled. They came off his tongue like a wind of blown chaff. He motioned Mitch to come closer with his finger, but Mitched stayed his ground. Wilson leaned off the car and stepped forward then, and the more Mitch watched and listened the more shriveled the man appeared. He was like a picture torn from the back page of a newspaper.

I know what people say behind my back. But what will you say? Anything? Are you mute? Can't speak. I could go on, you know. I could talk you down to your very knees. By then I'll be using grown up words, and those words will put a hole through your head, worse than this gadget, he said, turning the pistol.

Believe me I've done it.

He dropped the pistol at his side.

This isn't about me, now is it? Listen, I know why you came. It's about that game, isn't it? You said you beat it before. I don't doubt it. Year by year you've come and hit the bell and had your victory. But this year was different. They put the old dog on the game and he made it harder. He gave you a challenge for once, something that actually tested your strength, made you feel that all the power in the world ain't enough. And yet that's what you want now isn't it? To be tested. It's not about you coming this way to accost me, an old man. You've searched my jacket, you've searched my hat. You've accused me wrongly. I'm just an old man. And here I am trying to reason with you. But I don't mind. You see, this is about proving something to yourself. That old bronze tower is only a coverup. It wasn't enough to know you tried your best on a stupid little game. No, you had to prove it. You had to show something for it. Prove to people you're still strong. you made the bell ring, just like every year, that predictable victory you can claim without it being marred by anyone else. And you downplay it don't you? You even play mind games with yourself. You avoid looking at it. Pretend it's just a game, speak of it to others like you'd forgotten it was still here. But every year when you duck under those lights it's the first thing and last thing on your mind, isn't it. To round off your carnival. To come away with something. Not fritter away that money your mother gave you. Now isn't it? That's only my guess but I'll say so.

When he finished speaking he wiped his mouth with his gun hand like he was intoxicated with his own words. He laughed low to himself, and his laugh contained something novel now, an easygoingness. He was then self aware of the persuasion of his words, impressed by the sound of them, the upright logic and the psychological insight they evinced, how they subdued the large young man, tamed him into docility.

So think about what I said, Wilson said. Now I must be going.

He dropped the rope with the bears on it and waved the gun in a roundabout motion.

Now you get on too, he said. Enough of this.

Mitch turned halfway as if going, and Wilson turned to his car, and when he did Mitch sprang upon him like a loose coil and pinned him to the car. Wilson growled, pulled the trigger and the first two shots fired with a crack; BOOM, BOOM, but the next shots clicked. Blanks. Mitch tore the gun out of his hand and threw it behind, then he tossed the man to the ground like he were straw made, and mounted him, his hands fixing the geezer's wrists to the mud. Wilson writhed. His legs flailed and swept the dust. He looked like a wraith, a vampire. Close up Mitch saw the makeup that fell into the lines of his face as he twisted on his back, gibbering and whistling and snapping his teeth, unleashing a final, reckless assault of cusses and insults. Then he spit on Mitch's face and laughed. The laugh was not easy anymore.

Take your god'am hands off me you clumsy mute-

Then it stopped. Mitch came down on him. He struck the man's face into the earth three times. Heavy and swift. The first blow knocked two of his bottom teeth out. The second wiped him unconscious. The third snuffed his memory. In a rage Mitch raised the rock above Wilson's head and thought of finishing the act and the man right then, but he stopped when he heard his sister calling for him. He turned to the voice, lowered his hand, dropped the rock and stood up. He hovered over the man a moment, amazed that no sound came out of him. There was no sneer. He was unrecognizable. Mitch bent and searched Wilson's frock for the missing money but the pockets were empty. He peered in the van and saw nothing. The back was stuffed to the glass with animals. Finally he picked up the bears from the ground, and searching them over, he found a slit in the back of the last bear filled with wads of green crumpled bills. He pulled the stuffing out with the bills and it was a skimp animal. Then he cut it loose and took it back and returned the money. As for the game, it stood there waiting for him. The crowds were gone, the mallet was free, he had all the swings in the world. But he left it alone. He went away, and the bell never rang, and he was not bitter.

That night the stray chickens roamed as far as Wilson's van, and they clucked where he lay and pecked at his coat. Wilson woke in the black of night, when all the lights from the carnival were out. He was bewildered, and sitting up he quarreled with himself where he was or why he was sprawled to the dirt, why there with blood on his face, or blood in his mouth, why his hat was pummeled inside out, his bears ripped from one another; every sensation rising over him like a tide of evil he could not discern. He spit his teeth out on the ground and nearly cried, and when he recovered his senses he called the police, but they barely understood him because of the way his words sounded. Before they arrived he sat on the dust licking the gums between his teeth, thinking of what he would tell them when they came. And when at last he heard bells and sirens approaching he stroked mud through his hair and tore a sleeve from his coat and smeared spittle on his eyes for good measure. He made himself mewl and whelp. And when he believed they'd buy it he launched into his story of abuse and wrongdoing.

The View From Pier End

Down from the Chesapeake Bay, ducking under the Naval Academy Bridge and rounding past the city of Annapolis is a branch of water called the Severn River. And down from the Severn River, where the main body thins into a thousand scribbled creeks is a modest jut of beach called Cape Arthur Community Beach, where my family lives and where I spent my summers growing up. The layout hasn't changed much over time. There is one main beach and one main pier and both face out toward the mouth of the river and adjacent to a marked channel, where boats from both directions come and go. Families of ospreys live above the channel markers in big shaggy nests all year long. Beside the main pier, there is a strip of half-piers, a concrete boat ramp, and a makeshift diving board. The water over the diving board is slate-green, deep, and cold. You have goosebumps when you come out. Everywhere else, the water is olive brown. At the end of the main pier is a bench that no one sits on and a broad stretch of wood deck, good for sitting and watching and dangling legs over. On clear summer mornings the sun hangs over this spot in a yellow haze and looks as soft as the moon. The clouds are usually sheer and give the sky a chalky hue. When you sit down at low tide, you can look down and see the silty bottom of the river beneath your toes. The water's only a foot deep and it looks to be that shallow all around—to your left, to your right, behind you—way, way out even, as if the whole river were a single, sleek puddle meant for splashing.

During the summer when I was eleven years old I had little to do but eat, sleep and play, and I gave myself over to those activities with such abandonment that I became a tall order to my mother. My pleasure worried her. So did the length of day. She grew anxious at the thought of me "frittering away my energy on useless things." That summer she wanted me to be a grocery bagger, but I refused. I ran whenever she mentioned it. We had different agendas that summer and our different agendas put us at odds. She worked all day serving the family, and I worked all day serving my own adventures. Yet, she found savvy ways to recruit my help; she gave me outdoor chores, and assigned them in the morning so that the rest of the day was mine for the making. I trimmed tree branches, mowed the grass, washed windows, and chopped wood among other things.

I came to enjoy the mornings. Some mornings I got up early, when my father got up for work. I could hear him moving in the bedroom, whispering to my mother who was still half asleep. The house and hardwood floors were chilly, and the light that slanted through the blinds was blue. I ventured barefoot into the hallway listening for him, listening for his pacing, the brick-sound of his oxfords. My younger brother was still sleeping. Before he left, he'd wait until I put my flip flops on and followed him out to the car. The summer air outside was dewy and smelled of grass.

"Be good today." he'd say to me.

"I will."

Then he gave me a hug, the headlights came on, and off he went.

Goodness was his sole imperative to me, his one gentle proclamation over my day, and I never thought twice about it. Other mornings I was up before everyone else including my father. Those were my favorites. Those days I rose like an old man with an old habit. I felt that there was an elusive blessing in rising early, one that would vanish as soon as the sun came up. When I arose I went stirring around the house by myself, wandering into vacant rooms, delighting in my awakeness, boasting of it even. Sometimes I would climb atop my brother's bed and tease him awake, but often I became restive on my own and left the house and walked to the beach. It was a ten minute walk along a quiet back road. The houses on each side of the road receded into the thick coverage of evergreens. The trees stood high and formed a hallway of sorts, imposing a dense, vivid darkness on my path. I kicked pine needles along as I went and looked up with some relief at the moon shining in the ash-blue sky. My flip flops made a small, bright racket on the road, like a cricket chirping through high grass. The closer I got, the more the trees sparsed and revealed the first squib of water; a tiny back cove clinging to the river. The banks were shaded but the water in the middle reflected the sky. It was motionless, lovely to behold.

Before I reached the main gate I tried to listen for the sound of the water. If the water was calm, I heard hardly anything, perhaps ducks calling in the distance. If it was choppy, I heard the mush of boats shifting in their slips and the papery music of cordgrass bowing. If the water was rough, I heard the hollow clank of ropes and clips banging against masts and flagpoles. I listened as I moved. My ears primed my eyes with expectation, and when I opened the gate the slope of the hill tugged me forward and I sped down the gravel into the midst. I always walked along the water from one end of the peninsula to the other with my head held fast in front of me, like a sleuth in search of anything peculiar or enamoring. Except for a few fishermen gone for the morning, all the slips on the main pier were filled with boats of every kind; small and large, skiff and yacht, each one idly rocking and tethered to the stall like sleeping cattle.

At the end of the main pier I sat off the edge of the deck and watched the first scene of the day unfold. The world brightening gradually. The sun, the water and the banks beyond, every small motion they made accruing the beauty of mildness. The sun spread out like a fan and the river banks ahead were low and dark and bending. The water rolled steadily. The river went on as far as I could see in a single undivided course. Farther off, I imagined the river bleeding into the bay, and farther still the bay breaking into the sea. I inhaled this scene and never forgot it.

A few days per week I came and went like this, full of curiosity, then walked back home and waited for everyone else to get up. After my father, my mother woke next. She went straight from her bed to the kitchen and set a kettle brewing on the stove. She kept the noise down which guaranteed her a few extra minutes of quiet. When I came back, I heard her delicate clatter of spoon and saucer. I liked those sounds because they were the sounds of her awakeness. As she sipped her tea I came in and wished her 'Good morning', and she wished it back. I'd sit with her and we'd talk quietly for a bit. She'd make me breakfast. Often when we were talking she would look past me in a moment of reflection, with her mug at her lips, and then list off the chores I had that day. Before long she and I heard a few lone movements in the bedroom followed by a swift storm of feet scurrying to the kitchen. My mother shut her eyes, breathed long into the mug, and took a last, foreshortened sip.

In our family, there's me James and my brother Jude. We're a year and 10 months apart, both of us with dark brown hair, dark brown eyes and olive complexions. While Jude ate breakfast, I milled around the house waiting to hear what was going on that day; what errands were being run, who was going where, who was visiting whom. I moved from room to room toting a binder stuffed with football cards. I read and reread and shuffled them to no end. I put them into piles. I knew all the stats on the back of the cards. Then I put the binder away and played scales on the piano. Eventually my mother summoned me to the kitchen.

"James, I want you to mow the lawn this morning, ok?

Her tone of voice was businesslike, but cheerful, as if she already knew I'd do it. And I did. I gave her my word whatever she asked. She ran most of her errands in the morning and my brother with her. Sometimes she left him behind to help me with the chores, but often she took him with her to guard us from distraction. It was smart. When Jude stayed, we got distracted easily and early. We waited for her car to leave, then we dropped whatever task we started and raced to the shed to find the slingshot.

The slingshot. Nothing so beguiled us like the slingshot. Nothing so stirred envy and vainglorious competition between brothers like the slingshot. We lusted for it. My father bought it with the purpose of killing the squirrels that plundered his garden and apple tree. His plan was to eradicate a few of them in cold blood and leave them lying in the yard as a warning to the others. When it arrived in the mail, Jude and I practically knelt before our father and vowed our lives to help him carry out his mission. This slingshot was no fools device made of whittled wood and rubber band; It was a fully fledged weapon, designed to look and act like so. It was constructed from two polished spokes that branched into a Y, and a handle that gripped into the palm and strapped around the forearm for stability. The sling was a clear-yellow latex band that stretched back as far as you wanted and never broke. It came with ammo, a box of shiny metal ball bearings ready to be loaded. Unfortunately, the anticipation of shooting it blinded us from the reality that none of us knew how to shoot well. Within an hour, Jude and I learned that our father was (and would always be) a poor shot. It lent us a blow.

Most young boys assume their father is a good shot by nature, just as they assume their father is stronger than all the other fathers. With the slingshot, we hoped he would find his range eventually, but we were wrong. He never hit a squirrel. Once or twice he got close, but only close enough to frighten the squirrel to flee. It was no matter of effort. Every aim he took wrinkled his face into a mess of concentration and turned his eyes red. But he lacked calm, the steady eye behind the pouch. His shots sprayed across our yard and our neighbor's yard. They sprayed up into the trees, but nothing fell. Jude and I still stayed by his side like loyal hunt dogs, but over time our howls diminished. For a week we watched resignedly as the box of ammo went to waste. We ached to hold the weapon ourselves, but we kept quiet, careful not to clamor for it. In our home, clamor meant confiscation. So we let the fever build, and eventually we got our way. After a week, our father simply got tired of shooting. He got tired of missing, and his garden and tree were as bullied as ever. When he squibbed away his final shot he turned to us and said,

"It looks like I'm going to have to opt for a more practical solution to our problem."

His voice was low and relinquishing. He shook his head and led the way to the shed, cupping the slingshot in his hands like a dead sparrow, while we processed behind him dressed in mourning. He hung it on the wall, next to all the tools that failed their purpose. When he retreated to the house, Jude and I retreated too, only our eyes did not follow forward, but lingered behind us on the shed, on the spot where the slingshot hung, waiting.

We approached the shed again when our parents were gone on a Saturday afternoon, like mice returning to a pile of crumbs. We were as wary as the rodents too; full of pausing and going, turning and checking, desisting and persisting toward the doors. We feared getting caught, reproved, assigned some terrible work. The shed itself made us skittish too. It was a manifestation of my father's presence. His spirit loomed over it. He had built it and maintained it. Its very structure revealed him; the tattered shingled roof, the sturdy wooden walls and conservative coat of Nantucket grey. Even the orderly placement of tools inside conveyed him. Therefore we moved quickly inside. Jude stood guard while I ascended on my tiptoes and unhooked the slingshot off the wall. I brought it down nervously, picking it by its cold metallic limbs. A lump caught in my throat and Jude looked at me uneasily. I contemplated returning the slingshot when he raised a box of ammo and held it in the air between us. Our attention fixed on the small, flimsy box. I looked at him, unsure of what the gesture meant. He gave it a single shake, but I still did not understand. Then he jangled it again and again, and I stared at his shaking hand. I listened as the tiny pieces flew inside the container and the sound of metal on metal, going faster and faster, stirred like an angry bee hive. He stopped all of a sudden. The room went silent and we smirked and the air was stirring with rebellion.

Jude and I ditched our father's original mission and patrolled the woods behind our house instead. We shot for the hell of it. We hunted any object agreed upon, animate or inanimate, and took turns passing the slingshot until someone made contact or got close enough. We liked distant objects; birds high up in trees, a knot in a trunk for a bullseye, a vagrant squirrel. For practice we shot beer cans off the back fence by the woods. We would line up an empty dozen and fire until they all fell. Some were tipped over by a grazing shot, but the most satisfying were the dead-center shots, the ones that pierced the aluminum bellies with a SMACK. You could never stand those ones up again. For a while, the thrill of shooting spread over our arms like poison ivy. When we were shooting, our egos puffed and flagged. When we weren't shooting, we wanted to be. Our rules of sportsmanship were simple: A foul shot produced derision, and an average shot was ignored, it was worse than a foul shot. But in the event of a good shot, a really good shot, we marveled. We buckled over in silent disbelief, sometimes we laughed too. For some reason, brilliance was comedic. Perhaps it was because of the rarity of those shots, but I know now that Jude and I shot for those moments entirely. They made every miss worthwhile.

Since we were poor shots too, surrendering the weapon was the hardest part. As soon as we shot we wanted it back to reshoot, then the drama became waiting. While we waited we watched one another, and watchfulness was its own reward. The shooting itself was a beautiful, mesmerizing motion; one that seemed perfectly fitted for the charisma and body of a boy. I remember Jude's motion unmistakably; first him finding his shoulder-width stance and sturdying his feet to the earth. Then him placing a single ammo in the center of the pouch and pinching it shut. Like me, he was as skinny as a rail and his left arm wobbled as he drew the sling back. His back arched and as his eye narrowed on the target he bit his lower lip unconsciously. And then: release. Despite any errancy in aiming or precision, there was so much purity, so much straightforwardness in the release. Everything became untensed, destined. His face became normal again. We used the slingshot for a few weeks, off and on, improving little but shooting much. Our poor marksmanship was no dishonor though, and no dissuasion from shooting more. For one, accuracy meant less to us than motion, and the slingshot provided that in abundance. Secondly, we felt there was a tender relief in missing as much as we did, especially toward the animals we shot at. There was a real gladness in sparing something, even by our own unwit. We toyed with our consciences. We stalked every songbird inch by inch closer until it flew in fear. That was our whole adventure: toe the circle of guilt, but never step within.

Our slyness during that time was no match for our mother. She caught on early to our half done chores, and so consistently took Jude with her on her errands. The slingshot was no fun to use alone. I left it lying around the house and forgot about it. I did my chores complacently and looked forward to going to the beach in the afternoon. We all looked forward to going to the beach, including my mother. It was a boon to have her boys out of the home for a few hours. She stayed back and made tea while we marched along the back road like a pair of little pilgrims. Jude and I brought crab nets which we carried and used like staffs. Mine was tall and wood-handled with a warped head and emerald-green netting. Jude's net was short, black aluminum with a head big enough to hula hoop in. I carried a pail too for storing crabs. We avoided arriving at the beach directly at midday, since it was the hardest time to crab. The sun was relentless then, burning up your limbs and the sand beneath your soles. The wind whipped. The water was agitated. And most of the crabs were away. Only later they returned.

When we got to the main gate, Jude and I galloped down the hill lungs first and fled to different piers, anxious to raise the first filled net. We caught the crabs right off the pilings and never used cages or chicken legs or drove boats to find them. Seeing them was the first step. Whatever we learned about seeing we learned from our father, who often joined us at the beach after work. He taught us to search patiently; to be willing to get down to the edge of the deck on hands and knees and stomach, and scour every angle of piling before moving on to the next. The more we mimicked him, the more we noticed the give-away clues, the fleck of white underbelly, the jagged outline of shell, the bubbling mouth, the bluish gradient on a tucked claw. Whenever he spotted a big one we whooped and huddled behind him. I brought the pail close by, Jude squatted and watched. As we leaned forward to look we cast a bulky, three-headed shadow over the water. I loved watching my father's eyes, which were the closest to the water. Never have I seen them more intrepid than when they held their focus on a potential catch. He wore glasses too which gave his eyes a surgeon-like quality, a childlike intensity of seeing. I watched behind him through his own lens' to see what he saw, to watch the single-mindedness with which he brought the net patiently through the water. His glasses always slid to the end of his nose, but he somehow never lost them, and he never lost the crabs either. After a catch Jude and I became inspired to go and catch our own. We took our nets and raced to other parts of the pier. "Go slow!" he called out, but the words barely reached us.

Slowness came slowly. It was like unlearning boyhood and a thousand instincts. I lost every crab I rushed, hundreds over the length of the summer, but by the end I was stealthier. I could soft-step the pier the way one soft-steps hardwood floors avoiding squeaks. I could sprawl to the deck and start my net deep in the water, bringing it up without haste, letting the net billow. When the crab was totally encircled I captured it with one final yank. It was a mysterious and ecstatic thing to watch any creature break the surface of the water, but especially a crab, which looks like an alien to both worlds. It emerged from the water in a bout of fury. It threw its arms and beat its chest. I overturned the net and let it drop to the deck. If denied escape it tilted its body up, faced its transgressor, and held its arms open wide, willing to die. If provoked it pinched the rim of the net and did not let go until the arm broke and it fell back to the deck. Then it faced me again with its lone arm raised in a fist of injustice. For a moment my heart was racing. Racing and racing.

My father said the river was teeming with crabs that year. "Teeming"— what a glorious word. I wanted to explain teeming. To know it in my bones, to be it if I could. With each changing tide, the hours wasted wonderfully away and by the end of summer whatever time was left was swallowed up in our enjoyment of the days. The three of us, Jude and I and our father, returned to the house exhausted from our efforts. We were breathless and glad. The sun had kissed us. We could eat anything. Our cheeks were flushed, our shirts were stretched and damp at the hem. And our mother looked pleased to see us so tired. Silently she thanked the river. She fed us and loved us, and we slept soundly. The days moved slowly and perfectly, a lazy zag from one day to the next, from one end of summer to the other—until on one occasion the tether broke, and the perfect season snapped and fell apart.

I was up early that morning as usual. I waved my father off to work, walked to the beach and came home by the time my mother was awake. She was speaking on the phone, keeping her voice down.

"Yes. Yes. That works great. We'll be here."

When she hung up, I walked in, inquiring who it was.

"That was your Aunt Cassie. Her and Kurt are coming over today. I told her that Kurt could go crabbing with you and Jude." she said. I said nothing.

"Why, what's wrong with that?" she asked.

"Nothing, I guess."

"Alright, good, because I'm expecting you to be friendly to him."

Kurt was Aunt Cassie's son, my cousin. I left the kitchen trying to remember what I could about him, but it was vague, it had been a long time since we'd seen each other. I knew we were the same age. I knew he was shorter than me, a competitive wrestler, a tinier version of his father, Mike, who loved hunting.

"They'll be over after lunch." my mother added from the kitchen.

"If you all catch enough crabs we can eat them for dinner."

That cheered me up a bit. When Jude woke, we ate breakfast

then we tidied the backyard while my mother went to pick up food at the grocery. It was Friday, the coolest day of the week thus far. The sun shone behind thick clouds. When my mother returned she made us lunch and then we waited nervously until our guests arrived. They drove up at 2:30pm in a loud station wagon. The yellow hood was chipped and peeling. Aunt Cassie got out of the car and looked the same as I remembered, and Kurt got out after her. He was quiet. He had a buzzed head and wore a white tee and red shorts that went past his knees. He was chewing gum when he stepped out, chewing it in a slow cow-like way that gave his face a bored expression. We walked inside while he stayed behind and tied his shoe. When he came in, my mother asked him about wrestling but he didn't have much to say.

"It's good," he said. Then he shrugged his shoulders and looked around the room.

"How bout you boys go down to the pier and do some fishing and crabbing?" my mother asked.

"James, you can show Kurt where everything is, right?" I nodded.

Jude and I brought the nets, a pail and a fishing rod, and Kurt followed behind carrying the water jug and partly chatting with Jude. Neither of them was a natural talker, so between them was a dull exchange of short responses. I walked quicker to distance myself from their conversation but Kurt had to stop and tie his shoes again. We waited for him there on the road. The sun was out and it beat down so I could see the shiny redness of his scalp through his buzz cut. We kept going and soon we were at the entrance to the beach. None of us spoke while I opened the gate. When I opened it I trotted down to the bottom as usual, but Jude walked down with Kurt, who I heard asking where we caught the crabs.

"All over the pilings." Jude said

"That's dumb." Kurt replied.

I didn't hear Jude say anything after that. He took the fishing rod to one of the small piers and began casting and retrieving. He reeled with great control, as is to preserve the glassiness of the water's surface at that hour. I looked out on the still bay, waiting for something to stir it, for a fish to leap, or a stone to be skipped into the channel and ripple. Nearby I heard a loud commotion and I put my net down to see what it was. It was Kurt, three piers down from Jude. He was on his knees laughing and driving the net into the water like a spade. He slashed wildly as if he intended to make a scene. Jude came over too and we both realized that Kurt wasn't crabbing. We backed away and let him be. Jude went back to his fishing post and I went off to the main pier and started catching crabs. I caught one after another, all of them large. When I had half filled the pail, Kurt approached me from behind and looked into it. He lifted it and shook the crabs to rouse them.

"That's all? I thought you would've filled it by now." he said.

"It takes a while. You gotta go slow." I said without looking up. My eyes stayed fixed on the water and I tried to ignore his presence. He walked away, dragging his feet to enunciate himself and his boredom. Out of my periphery I saw him bent over, searching the pilings. I heard his net plunge and emerge twice, empty each time. I tried to ignore him but his futility angered me, and whatever he was mumbling under his breath began to itch in my ear and drive me crazy. I imagined him saying "stupid, stupid, stupid", repeating it like some mantra or prayer. From what I knew of him, that was the melting point of everything—stupidity. I felt unfree when he was near me, self-conscious of my own enjoyment. He could have left, but didn't and instead he lingered around looking miserable. In my thoughts I applied a cold pity to him and kept my distance. I left the main pier and snuck around the back inlets of our beach to spots where he would never find me. I made myself invisible and bitter and the bucket filled quickly.

When it filled all the way we left. We gathered silently at the gate and walked back faster than we came, in some kind of false hurry. I hugged the bucket up to my chest to keep it from swaying into my legs and slowing me down. The crabs were under my chin, all of them piled flat, none of them panicked or fighting now. Their arms were tucked. Their mouths bubbled innocently. But for the first time I felt utter indifference toward them. Just crabs, stupid crabs, I thought. That sentence lodged in my mind and the longer it stayed the more it fed the disdain growing within me. I wanted to put the pail down, it was getting heavier and heavier. When we got home I walked straight through the front door to the kitchen and lifted it onto the counter. My mother and aunt were drinking coffee at the table. Kurt and Jude followed in.

"Well, how'd it go?" my mother asked.

"Good." we said with one voice.

We showed them the crabs and they were surprised. We did not mention who caught them.

"Very impressed, guys. Good work. We'll cook some of these later. Sorry Dad couldn't join you today. He's running late. You three go and find something else to keep you busy." my mother said. Her and my aunt continued talking. As I walked to my room I heard her say

"They're awful quiet. They must be tired from catching all those crabs."

"I guess so." my aunt replied.

I sat in my room for half an hour laying football cards on the ground and organizing them into piles. It was relaxing and at least I could do it in quiet, without being disturbed. When I got bored I came out to check and see where everyone was. The hallway to the kitchen was beginning to smell like Old Bay. The big silver pot on the stove was wafting warm steam on the front burner, billow by billow. The aroma spread into the other rooms. A few of the windows in the dining room were opened and letting in a cool breeze. I could hear the muffled voices of Kurt and Jude coming from somewhere. Their voices were intermittent with a soft thumping sound, a sound like a finger flicking a cantaloupe. From the living room I saw them standing in the front yard, a few feet from the driveway. The main door was open, the screen door cracked. When I walked outside, their backs were turned to me and the crab pail was below them at their feet. Jude wore a strange look on his face, his arms were crossed.

Kurt held something in his hands and as he drew his arm back the metallic bits of slingshot glimmered off his forearm. He aimed over the opening of the pail, the sling was wire thin. Then he released. Whatever ammo he used did not ricochet off the bottom or sides, but fired into something and stayed stuck. Thump. Thump. Again and again. He stooped and grabbed a handful of stones from our driveway and placed one in the sling pouch. Dumbfounded, I moved closer and watched him shoot again, as if it were something I had never seen before. He kept the pail pinned under his eyes. Between shots, he glanced back at me to summon me closer still. Small runnels of sweat fell from his temples down the side of his face, and some sweat accumulated on his upper lip. When I was close enough

I looked over the ledge of the pail, frozen in all my abilities but observation.

He shot two more times, each time a good shot. Inside were the unused crabs, about 8 of them if you counted up all the pieces. A brown putrid layer of fluid sat at the bottom of the pail. Finally, he threw the slingshot on the ground and hunched forward to evaluate his shots. He looked simultaneously pleased and bored. Then he started to laugh, then Jude started to laugh, then I joined in, caught up in the bondage of a horrible chorus. Our noise resounded with the same shrill, unbroken voice. When Kurt stopped laughing he turned calmly and walked back to the house, brushing the slingshot into the yard with the outside of his foot. Jude followed him without a word, only I remained.

I stood loitering by the pail, hating it, bewildered by it, and yet drawn to the mess inside. It smelled terribly. I was waving flies from over the top when my father pulled into the driveway and got out of the car.

"What's going on, James?" he asked, noticing me there.

"What did you do?"

"Nothing." I muttered.

He came over, took one glance into the pail then jerked his face back from the smell. He turned and saw the slingshot in the yard then turned back to me, but I could not look him in the face. I kept swatting at the flies to avoid his attention. He continued looking at me. He held his satchel in one hand and his blazer draped over his forearm and breathed stiffly through his nostrils. His silence pried into my conscience like a crowbar. Still, I had nothing to say. I was empty of any desire to blurt the names Kurt! Jude! After my long unresponsiveness, he departed from me and went inside.

When he left, I stared at the pail until the look of it infuriated me. I lifted it off the ground once more. Its weight had left a circular depression in the grass. I took it and started walking toward the beach, intent on putting it away for good. I closed up. I buffeted myself from feeling any jabs of remorse and shrugged along. I was staffless, pail-heavy, and imbalanced by the rot weight digging into my grip. Every few strides the swinging pail knocked against my shin or calf and left a scrape. It hurt, and yet it pleased me in a strange way too, like I was exposing myself to an austere and necessary justice.

Soon I heard the sound of the water and when I stopped I smelled the swish of blood-water beside me. When I opened the gate I did not run as usual but stepped shyly at the slope and descended. For the first time there at the bottom I felt nothing toward the water. No curiosity, no desire to find crabs. I did not want to see them or be seen with them. I wanted to be rid of the ones I had brought. I stayed off the main beachfront and walked along the back creek of the river where the concrete boat ramp slid down into the water. The water was rustling and bright with a cloudy green tint. I was alone. On the half pier parallel to the ramp I got down on my knees and put the pail beside me.

One last time I looked in. The shells on top were jeweled with the stones that broke them. I stopped looking, sprawled to my belly, and held the bucket out over the face of the water. An instant of hysteria rushed me as I lowered it - I expected something to happen, for the water to tremble or boil at my offering, but it never did. I tilted the pail and the remains slid out in a wet lump of shards, barely disturbing the surface. The stones sank quickly, but the shells sank slow, tumbling through prisms of light and deconstructing like ornate puzzle pieces. I knelt and watched until the last bit buried in the silt, then I took the pail and came to my feet. The sun was going down but I did not want to go home yet. I walked to the main pier and looked out at the distant part of the river, the part where it broadened into deeper water. Then I walked on, watching the water pass under my feet under the boards.

I walked straightforwardly, not once veering to lean my head over a piling, and at the end I sat down on the bench where no one sits and dragged the empty pail in front of my feet. I placed my hands over my knees and inhaled slightly. Then I wailed with all my might until the outburst flushed my face and made me dizzy. I felt the hoarseness in my throat. My head wilted in front of me where I saw the water. From the reflection I caught the late sun sending a red streak through the clouds into the continuous play of shadow, glint and wave off the end of the dock. The view was like looking at one great, watery ember.

I looked down at my body and regarded how puny it was, how insubstantial; the bonyness, the blister on my belly, the scraped shins, the curl of my toes. I wanted a cloak to cover my skin, and another cloak to rend with my hands from top to bottom. I wanted to make an ultimatum, to commit myself to some real hatred of this place. But I could not. The scene carried on, tireless in its pulchritude. Along the shore I heard the splashing of waves and children's laughter. The sky was big and clear, the color of forgetfulness. The sun was saying goodbye, the boats and wind were chiming. The river was broadening and branching, being as it always was, lovely and crooked. Under my sternum I felt an ugly pain. I walked back to the start of the pier, then I rinsed the pail and walked home.

Night Fever

From the first moment they walked through a strange door and laid hands on someone else's belongings they felt the intrusiveness of their presence. The feeling was not always sudden or immediately palpable, but subtly it occurred to them, when a house was being pared away of all that made it a home; the particularity of its layout, its niches and play corners being disassembled at their hands, the table on its back, every cabinet opened in the kitchen - the children whispering to themselves, wondering who it was that took their things. And who could not feel the infringement? Who could not sense that moving anything at all, let alone places where people lived required a double sensitivity; straightforwardness yet tenderness, muscle yet delicacy?

Randy and Michael were movers. They were best friends who met in college and started a company after graduation called Ace Moving Co. near Annapolis, Maryland. They were five years in. Two years prior they had purchased a used big white moving truck, scraped the old decal off and replaced it with their own. They ran their whole operation out of the truck. Randy was the unofficial leader of the two; taller, stronger, better with people. He had a goatee and short stiff hair that stood without his trying. Michael was a head shorter, and unlike his partner, couldn't move anything alone. But the men depended on one another; they were each other's arms and legs.

Moving was a chastening job; for two men it involved their whole selves, requiring as many social virtues as it did physical exertion. Once, early on, they helped move a recently divorced woman who owned hundreds of books. Between trips, Michael, who was holding a box of books, rolled his eyes and said to Randy under his breath,

"I guess she needs something to keep her busy."

The woman, who was nearby, overheard him and said

"Give me that." wrenching the box from his arms

He said "I'm sorry, let me take that. I can get that."

She said "Shut your mouth and do your job and keep your comments to yourself."

Then she carried it off; a box heavy enough to break her. They had moved most things under the sun. The objects people could not bring they left behind. Randy and Michael's bachelor house became a boneyard of unwanted furniture, most of which they did not know what to do with. But one piece was their favorite. They acquired it years ago. An elderly couple downsizing to a smaller house hired them and packed most of their belongings in boxes, but left in the living room a La Z Boy couch, ink colored, rumpled, worn down at the head and arm rests where the man and his wife sat for years. When Randy and Michael went to move it, the old man reached his hand and said,

'Not yet. We don't want to move this yet. I'm still not sure if it's coming." He put his hand on the back, patting it, and fell quiet. Like the touch gave him a sad thought. So they let it be. All day the men stepped around. Finally the old man's wife, looking at it said

'I think it needs to stay. We've worn it out.' He nodded. Then they moved it.

In time they learned that good work was a matter of care. It couldn't be rushed or half heartedly gone about. What they gave significance to, even the details of packing lamps or putting screws in plastic baggies, had the effect of returning significance to them. They became the quality of their work.

Now it was summer, moving season, when they hired the kid, because they needed an extra set of hands. The staircase was stuffed with heat. Body heat; heat-heat; heat coming off the wood steps and rails. Backwards and forwards they went, moving as one, scuffing and shuffling, feet staggered on the stairs, couch weight lugging down their shoulders near out of socket; all of it toilsome, except for Evan, the kid they hired, who stood by like a lame shadow, yawning. His eyes were deep set and slumberous. 'You're good, you're good', was all he said, making sure they didn't trip over anything, but otherwise offering no assistance. At the base of the stairs, Randy lifted from bottom, his brown hair sticking above the bulk of armrest he was under. His face was red. The gold necklace he wore at all times fumbled out of his shirt. He cussed. Said 'wait!' to Michael on the other end, steadied the frame on his thigh, blew a breath out, 'k!', climbed. Michael back stepped slowly to the top, then they sidled through the hallway. The kid clunked behind.

The woman whose belongings they were moving lifted her cat out of the way and watched from an empty door frame as they lowered the couch a little to the left, a little more, a little back, perfect. As soon as it was placed the cat leapt onto the cushions, stretched out and slept. Randy said 'I understand that feeling.', put his necklace back, and wiped his nose with his sleeve. Then he went to carry more things. The kid was outside checking his watch and fanning himself by the time they came to take another load.

"How much more we got?" the kid asked.

"How much more is back there? We've still got four or five more trips, don't we?" Randy replied.

"I haven't checked yet."

"We leave when everything's unloaded. Until then we keep at it."

The kid sighed grudgingly but never bothered to check for himself. The thought of the work drained him. He walked around the boxes left by the truck and nudged them with his foot, feeling their weight. He took the light ones on his way back up; the half filled, or hardly filled ones, and sometimes none at all, but would follow behind the others as they carried, waiting to pick up any little thing that might drop while they were going.

Randy said to Michael privately "Good grief. I don't know what to do with him. He doesn't put his back into anything, and I can't force him.

"We've only got him for a few more weeks." Michael said.

"Then we make sure we give him something to do."

That afternoon things came together despite the persistent slovenliness of the kid, who avoided anything strenuous. The men worked around him, quietly, diligently, arms full of cabinets, mirrors, and end tables, until nothing remained in the truck but straps and dollies. It was a good sight to see, the empty truck. The look of completion. When all was finished,

Michael stepped in, as was his custom and swept all the dust out the back with a work broom.

Before they left, the woman thanked Randy for their work.

'Do you need anything else?' she asked.

'Just a good referral' Randy said.

Then they drove off, Michael in the passenger and the kid in the back drinking from the water jug. He wiped his mouth and held the jug between his thighs until they dropped him off.

Randy unrolled his window and spoke out,

"Tomorrow we're at it again. We'll be here at 7 to pick you up."

But Evan made no outward gesture of acknowledgement. The men watched him as he went up to the door of his parent's house, walking as he had the whole day long. Then they went home too, tuckered out, too tired to complain even, the straps of their back braces falling off their shoulders.

Evan was a kid from town, a lanky unambitious college student who answered their ad in the paper and said over the phone that he was a hard worker; and they believed him. But a month of work proved otherwise, and with only two weeks left in their agreement, nor many jobs remaining, they resigned themselves to whatever he could do. He was mostly company.

One morning they were working a move in the country, loading their truck with rusty farm equipment from a barn. The client was a retired farmer who sat in the shade of his yard in a lawn chair, cocking his hat up and down, watching them. The day burned. Not a cloud in the sky.

They planned to break at noon. At 11 Randy had two bags of cement mix hung on his shoulder. From afar Michael heard Randy say "Ahh", a pained sound, not loud, but pronounced enough that he turned to see what was the matter. When he turned, Randy was kneeling beside a bag of cement on the ground which had broken open. He ran over.

"How you doing, partner?" Michael said.

Randy exhaled heavily.

"You all right?"

Randy nodded,

"I just need a break." Randy said. With Michael's arm he stood to his feet and walked lethargically to the truck. He pulled a cigarette from the front seat, lit it and sat down on the ledge of the lawn. The grass was warm under his palm. He leaned to his elbow, glared up briefly at the sun, then made a visor with his hand. "Take it easy." Michael said, then he went back to work. Evan! he yelled. Evan! He looked around, searching for the kid, who finally came from behind the barn holding the water jug.

"Yeah?"

"Where have you been?

"Nowhere." he said.

"Put that down and hold these straight while I bind them."

There was a stack of rebar on the ground in a pile. The kid put his foot on it clumsily.

"Come on, that won't do. Get closer. Get on your hands and knees, and keep it down. Otherwise I won't be able to bind it tight enough, and all this is gonna spill out when the truck's moving. It's heavy, I don't want that coming loose. Feel that? You've got your work gloves don't you?" Evan pulled the gloves he was given from his back pocket and put them on.

As Michael was binding the poles together he heard a squeak and a movement. The farmer had folded his chair and came over to them.

"I think your friend's sleeping." he said.

"Sleeping? who?"

"Your friend," he said, pointing, "He took a nap looks like."

Michael looked up and saw Randy beside the truck, flat on his back. His legs swayed, standing only by the triangle they formed with the ground. Then they collapsed in front of him.

"Randy! Randy!" he yelled, dropping what he held and sprinting to his friend. He called louder and more bewildered. The kid stood there, his gloves still on, frozen like. Michael bent down and took his friend by the face saying "Randy, look at me, look at me" He moved his face side to side, trying to make eye contact, but the head bobbed aimlessly. He took Randy's hand which had fallen by his side and shook it lightly, feeling nothing but the limb's own looseness.

"Randy!" he said, "Randy, randy…. randy" he called, his voice rising, lowering. He turned to the kid "Get up! Get that water! Quick!" He yelled to the old man "Call 911. My friend's in bad shape."

"Hang in there, Randy." Randy's jaw moved slightly. His neck turned limply, and he slurred something.

"What'd you say? I'm here, I'm here."

He grabbed the jug blindly from the kid and shook it desperately when he felt it. "It's empty! Grief! he said, shaking it some more. He tipped the nozzle over Randy's lips till water ebbed out, but it was not much, and it merely skimmed off, leaving a clear, ice cold runnel running down his jaw off his neck.

"Get more! We need more!" The kid took the jug and went off, but it was no use because he did not know where to go.

Randy's lips became stiff and dry while they waited. Then his eyes stopped rolling. Then he let out one final meek breath from his nostrils and expired. The body went still. Michael put his head to the man's chest and his hands fell to the lawn, clenching the grass. He shut his eyes hard to dam the tears, to dam the fury of his thoughts, but he could not hold them back. He sobbed into his friend's shirt, shaking with weakness. When he had stopped, he opened his eyes, blurry, rubbed them dry, and braced his hands on the ground to stand, hitting the kid's shoe instead, who had been standing there. The foot moved back. Michael looked up and saw him extending the full jug of water.

Randy died of a heat stroke, they learned. The town received news. That week Michael sat despondent in the apartment where he and Randy lived. The rest of the moving jobs were canceled and when the kid called asking about pay, he did not respond. He pushed all the furniture against the walls except Randy's couch, which he left in the middle of the floor, not wanting to touch it. Its solitary presence intensified the absence of his friend.

When he left the apartment he visited Randy's parents in Davidsonville, in the country. He had known them for a long time. They were like family. They lived in a modest one storey house, near the end of a bumpy gravel road, surrounded on all sides by fields of tall crops. Randy's parents were making preparations for the funeral. Michael walked in and sat down in the living room, shaking hands with the father and hugging the mother.

The house was silent but for their talking plans, though even that was spoken with a hush, with a restrained formality. The father was a farmer, but that day he was dressed in a white button down and slacks. His hair was combed to the side. He looked like another man. When Michael came they took a break; Randy's father pulled out a day's old newspaper tucked into the side of the chair and rapped it idly on his thigh, then offered it to Michael, who skimmed the headlines then returned it. The wife prepared snacks. She came with a tray of food and set it down on the table in front of the tv.

"There's cokes in the garage as you know. I didn't know which one you wanted."

She returned to the kitchen while Michael and the father ate.

When they finished she came to pick up the tray, and she hesitated slightly, turning back to Michael.

"Michael," she said. "I wonder if you'll do something for me?"

She glanced aside at her husband and corrected herself "Something for *us*, actually." There was some apology in her voice.

"Of course." Michael said. "What is it?"

The father looked up at her, like it was news to him too what she was going to ask.

"I want to light a candle for Randy sometime, and maybe you can help. Years ago we went to a church downtown called St. Christophers, where they've got stands of candles on the sides of the church, where people come and kneel and offer prayers for their loved ones. Do you know the church?

"I don't think so."

"It's not far from where you live. When you go by it, you'll know it I bet. Big wooden doors; old looking. Ever since Randy passed I've had that on my mind to do. You know, to keep something alive for him; a memorial, besides his tombstone of course."

She stood quiet a moment, the thought quickly overtaking her with sadness. She dried her eyes with a napkin off the tray and regained control of her voice.

"There's no place around here that has it. They can't do it at the viewing or the funeral. I've already asked. The home director and the pastor said that wasn't part of their service. It's too bad. But I know St. Christopher's does, and we grew up taking the family there when we lived closer to town. We'd have gone ourselves, but we've got family coming into town soon, and with all the preparations we haven't found a moment."

"I'm happy to go." he said "It's not a problem."

"It's just been on my mind," she said. "And I suppose it doesn't have to be that exactly."

Her husband spoke up,

"Now what do you mean it doesn't have to be that exactly? Let's keep it simple for him. One thing's enough for now. You had a good idea; now let him do it, and if he's got any other ideas for remembering Randy I'm sure he'll get to it. But your idea is a good one, and he'll do that first thing."

She looked off considering the words, thinking to herself, with the tray on her hip. Then she looked back at Michael.

"You'll know the best thing. You were a brother to Randy. You've been a son to us. It'd mean the same thing either way. You may even have something better in mind."

"I appreciate it," he said. "It'll be no problem stopping by the church."

"Thank you." she said. "It's small, but it means a lot to us."

"You'll do good." the father said.

The mother smiled, took the tray to the kitchen, and came back with a note with the church's address on it. She gave that to him, then she put a folded bill in his hand.

"You can put that in the offer box when you go." she said.

It was around midday then. After a while Michael got up and walked outside for fresh air.

He walked through the barn and along the gravel road. The land was green, fragrant with plant life and dried crumbled earth. Randy's father caught up with him, pointing out what was what on the property, what the crops were doing, what the weather had been lately, many little intimate details, that combined, were more than the man had spoken in all their previous meetings. Michael asked questions; questions he didn't so much care the answer for, as much as he wanted to prolong the rambling, which was good and light minded. It had innocence to it. Thus they spoke about a good deal; they walked and rambled. Yet their words, whatever they talked about, did not mention their one great loss.

Randy's father pointed halfway down the field on the left.

"You see that squib of stubble?"

"Yeah."

"That's just hay I rake over nowadays. Nothing grows on that spot."

"Why not?"

"Years ago I spilled a heap of fertilizer on it accidentally. The rig I was using to spray with broke as I was taking it across with the tractor and gushed out in that one patch. I didn't catch it till the next day, after it rained. The dirt was soaked with rain and up comes this thin layer of bright green slime sitting on top. It looked like antifreeze. It just came up, bubbling almost, like the ground was spitting it up. I've cleared it since, but it does no good." He pulled out a crumpled box of cigarettes from his pocket, stuck one between his lips and gave another to Michael. They walked back smoking.

The viewing and funeral happened the same week. He looked long at the body in the casket, less with sorrow than with strained recognition. The waxy complexion, the smoothed hair, the silk tie; every neat detail misgave him for the man he knew. He and seven other white gloved pallbearers processed into the cramped country church carrying the deceased. An eerie, unsettling sensation came over him lifting the dead man he had spent most of his days lifting dead weight with, and the sensation did not dissipate suddenly upon putting the casket down and sitting, but lingered yet; for neither his mind nor his heart was a pure vessel of grief, however much he desired so; each contained instead an admixture of serious and irrelevant thoughts, distractions, contemplations of the future, previous regrets, including not least the thought of the kid, who hadn't come to pay his respects, and who's image stole like an imposter thought into the privacy of the moment. It was the image of the face especially, that would not budge. The profound boredom in the eyes. The succession of yawns. The thought of him standing there with the water extended, while Randy passed, or waiting in the shade of the truck for the day's work to be done, as he had done many times. It was an unfortunate way to remember his friend by, Michael thought. Still more episodes recalled themselves, ebbing and swirling through the course of eulogies, the cumulation of which hindered the act of cherishing the man's memory. A certain guilt prevailed over Michael that hour, for however much he wanted to, he could not mourn.

It was only the mother's look at the end of the proceedings that gave him relief and pulled him out of his thoughtfulness. She saw him from afar and came over, hugged him, and thanked him for coming. As she pulled him close to give him one last hug, she said

"Remember that favor."

"I will," he said.

"I know you will."

Then she smiled, gave him a kiss on the cheek and let him go.

The next day, when the favor was still in his mind, Michael followed the address he was given toward St. Christopher's church not far from where he lived. It was on a street he had never been to. Surveying its facade as he drew closer, it was obvious he had never seen it straight on, but only ever out of the corner of his eye or from afar. Its enormity loomed upon him for the first time standing before it- the building's height not proving the sole impressiveness of its structure; rather its girth, its solidity, the weight of all its stone bearing on the very look of it. Next to the church was an abandoned parking lot on one side and a row of small suburban houses on the other so that everything in proximity looked flattened by comparison.

It was an old weathered place; two grandfather oaks stood on the same plot of land, equal in age to the church and sharing with each other a similar lofty, sagely stature. Their roots bulged profusely underground, lifting the entrance sidewalk in spots, poking here and there above the earth, and running like so all the way to the roadside fence, where another protrusion tilted the spoke gate backward so much that the door swung open of its own will and could not close without assistance. This, and all outward elements contributed a look of unevenness throughout the place. Moss and ivy clambered low along the base of the church and flourished except in one spot near the side door where a few shreds had been torn by hand, but was quickly being overtaken with new growth, the verdant summer seizing upon it.

Michael walked steadily on, the lone pilgrim at that hour. Everywhere his eye glanced was the evidence of some patchwork of old and new stone, of some structural fortification or item under repair. Though downtrodden in corners, the church on the whole was not uncomely and not nearly unwelcome, for it commended a different kind of appeal, largeness and humbleness both; the kind of appeal apparent in good furniture- when age has not made them less useful but more. And it remained as it had been founded; a house of praise, a lonely kind of refuge.

There were two slits of unilluminated stained glass near the top of the church facing the side he entered at, looking upon him as he came to the doors like two vacant eyes. He entered upon a side foyer. The church was dim then, with a memorable dampness, and a damp smell too. The walls on the inside were wood paneled and as the church opened into the main sanctuary they became the stones he had seen from the outside. An organist was practicing somewhere he could not see. There was a large sign just inside the sanctuary that said "Night Fever: prayer vigil", and beside it on a table was a woven basket filled with green discarded pamphlets that said "Night Fever: prayers and benediction", dated from the night before. He picked one up and put it down. On another table was a second basket with spent tea candles, seemingly burned the same night, and beside that too was a candle stand that had been moved to the back with nothing in it but old wax.

He entered the sanctuary peering around through the dimness for the permanent candle stands like the ones Randy's mother had described. On the side he stood there was one such area, but it was roped off and dark, and he saw that it was the place where the stand in the foyer had been moved from. There were statues he could not make out and an offering box attached to the wall. He walked along the back of the church, straight on to the other side, where the only other light except above the altar area, came from. There was one other person in the church, a woman he saw from afar who went by collecting old green pamphlets in the pews and putting them in a cardboard box.

Near the other side Michael saw the candlelights burning in a stand and behind the stand was a wooden statue of a man holding the Christ child on his shoulder. He put the money he was given in the offering box and came forward taking a stick to light a candle with, yet there was nowhere to light. Every candle was burning already. He went up and down the columns searching against his first impression, but it was true that none remained. He looked a third time and the same. Each candle burned peaceably and steadily but one, he had barely seen it, in the corner. It was a troubled flame, the kind that burns inconsistently, consuming too much wick and sputtering away, and he had the temptation right then and there to snuff the unruly thing. He wondered if it would die as he watched it, and if so, if he should light it again, or if it would vanquish just as soon; thus he queried with himself and stayed a whole minute observing it alone, desiring it to falter so he could finish the favor, but it burned defiantly; not just the one, but all of them so long as he watched. Finally he turned and left, stumped by circumstances, wondering why the world holds out in such queer ways sometimes.

Outside the sun was shining, the back door bright with good weather, and all around him, harmonious with the organ practicing, the stained glass windows flushed with color in one gradual transposition so that glancing over the once dim sanctuary was like looking over a new church altogether, so filled had it become by warmness. In the back foyer before leaving he stopped idly and took a green pamphlet from the basket, a more or less thoughtless gesture, but something he thought he might share with Randy's mother as a proof of his visit. The woman who was collecting them in a box came by as he was standing.

"You're free to keep that one." she said "It's from last night, but we use the same prayers every month."

She was an older woman. She wore a long sleeved blouse and a skirt that broke just above her ankles when she walked.

"Thank you," he said. "Do you know if there's other candles in the church to light for someone? There's none available on the other side."

"Unfortunately no." she said. "We have just the one side right now. I'll replace this other stand back later today. We had our monthly prayer vigil last night and we moved this one up to the front of the church for that, so it's out of place for the moment. I'm sorry." she said.

"That's alright, I can come back another time."

"You're more than welcome."

With those words he had moved to the doors and was standing in the big wooden door frame, ready to go out, his raised arm propping it open.

"Besides," she added, "it's the intention that counts. Every prayer is heard even if you couldn't light a candle today. It's not the candle, you know, it's the heart."

"The heart," he said, considering the words to himself, "Thank you."

As he left a strong draft from outside swept across his body and into the church. He waved her goodbye, the pamphlet fluttering between his fingers.

He made no plans to go back soon. All day the incompleteness of the errand hung over him, and the days following continued. Whatever *heart* he may have shown by accepting a favor did not require the reality of leaving it unfinished. He appeased his misgivings by taking Randy's belongings gradually out of the apartment; some he returned to the parents; some he gave to the Salvation Army. Other things, bigger things, he kept around. His friend's gold necklace he found coiled in a small pile on a bookshelf where he had placed it the same day Randy passed. He wore it to keep it from getting lost while he boxed books. Besides, it was a small chain, not worth the pawning. All of it; the cleaning and the boxing and the necklace, were small acts to get him through. They comprised the ritualism of his grief.

Meanwhile the favor never left his mind, but engrossed as it persisted. He felt that the forgone days between his visit to the church and now, as well as his sluggishness returning, were a kind of accrued dishonesty adding to the cost of the favor- at least, that the favor was not nominally the mother's anymore, but assuredly his too, and that whatever he should do in recompense should involve a price steeper than lighting a candle in a close space. For days he pondered. The green pamphlet he took remained on the front floor of the truck, so consciously or not, he read the words 'Night fever' every time he got in or out until the phrase was lodged in his mind, fanning his imagination. Soon the smoke was rising. He had conceived an idea and now the plan was stirring in his mind.

It was not happenstance when the kid called again, the next

day, asking for payment.

Michael said 'I can pay you, but I have one job left for us to do.' The kid agreed. He came over late in the afternoon and they began by clearing Michael's apartment of all the leftover stuff, all the furniture, putting everything in the truck.

"What are you doing with all this?" the kid said.

"Clearing it." Michael replied, lifting one end of the couch impatiently until the boy picked up the other, then walked hard forward, forcing the kid backward. Once they had it on the ledge of the truck, Michael nudged Evan aside and shoved it to the back, real hard.

"You're getting rid of all this stuff? Whose is it?

"Not mine."

"Then why do you have it?"

"I ended up with it."

"It's still in good shape though."

Michael turned hard on his heel toward the kid. "That's not the point," he said, and flung the load of scrap wood he was holding into the bed of the truck.

"You don't want to give it away instead?"

"I'd prefer to not keep answering questions right now." he replied, then nodded to a chair still unloaded. "Now take that end…"

When they finished it was after 8. Michael was exhausted from having loaded most of the truck himself. He told the kid to hop in the back seat and they left.

"Where are we going?" the kid asked.

"To a memorial."

"For Randy?"

"Yes."

"Where?"

But he did not say.

"You might have to move some things around in the back," he said instead.

When the kid climbed in the backseat he pushed aside a plastic bag and propped his feet on top of two stacked shovels face down on the floor.

"Just keep those under your feet." Michael said.

In the cramped space the kid sat with his arms folded and his eyes moving around the cabin and out the window. On their way to wherever they were going they stopped at a gas station and Michael took a red can from the back of the truck and filled it.

They drove out of town into the country, where the only homes were separated by strict plots of farmland and austerely lit. The truck slowed and turned onto a dirt road, the change in pavement kicking up rocks that bounced under the vehicle, and loose cargo went scraping and sliding in the truck bed. The kid sat up, looking over the driver's shoulder to see where they went. Now and then he caught the bright moon in the periphery of his side window, following them like a patient, watchful eye through the thicket of stalks. It was nearly full. They passed many rows of crops, drawing closer to a small lit house in whose direction they drove dead on, but they stopped before and parked by a clearing where the earth was low and stubbled, and the stubble glinted with the moon.

When they got out, Michael left his door open and said "Can you grab those two shovels?" He walked into the middle of the clearing, then paused, putting his thumb in a belt loop, and looked around, surveying the ground; then he turned to the kid who had dragged the shovels in each hand behind him across the field to the spot where he stood. He motioned for one and he gave it to him, and he walked over the ground with it, steady, and finally punched the sharp tip into the ground and laid his foot on it so it stood. "Take that other one and leave it be right now." The kid, imitating Michael, laid his foot on the blade heavy, till it stuck in the ground.

"Come with me." Michael said. Out in the distance, beyond the dark enclosure of the crops they heard a howl, clear and sad. He led the kid to the truck and unlatched it and threw it open. The two stood looking at the dark shapes they had loaded earlier that day.

"What are we doing?" Evan asked in his usual resistant tone.

Michael shook his head and took a lunging step into the truck bed, ducking his head under the latch.

"Just help me unload." He stepped into the cavernous inside and emerged with an armful of scrap wood, handing the load to Evan.

"Put it over there, where the shovels are."

"Anywhere?" the kid asked.

"Anywhere. In a pile."

When the kid came back Michael handed him pallets, then drawers, then shelves. One by one he piled them. Michael heard them bashing together. The kid came back breathing heavily. Then Michael gave him cushions, table legs, armchairs; he put them into the kid's arms forcibly. There were no words for a long while. The kid, very gradually, had stopped speaking to conserve his breath and now there was only the sound of feet along the ground, thuds of wood, exhales. The kid came and went, but there was something in his movement Michael had not seen before.

Last of all Michael stepped down and said to the kid "Now you go up and push the bottom half of that couch to me." It was the last thing left; Randy's couch, the La Z Boy; a hunk of cloth and wood with a pull-out bed inside. Evan got into the truck, and pushing hard, shimmied it off the edge into Michael's grip, then got down and grappled the other end. It was heavy and slow carrying, slower even because of the dark. They lifted it to the middle of the heap, and erected it on its side, high above the rest of the heap, leaning against it for support. It was imbalanced when it stood and made a sprung whining sound, the inside being jostled.

They peeled the cushions off, revealing the big tear in the middle and exposing the sinuous, black metal frame of the bed. Michael went to the truck and returned with stacks of newspaper and gas. He portioned a stack of newspaper and gave it to Evan, then made another for himself.

"What are we doing?" the kid said, the trepidation filling his voice "Are we allowed to be here? He shied one step back.

"More than alright." he said.

"Is this for a fire?"

Michael had a stack of newspapers extended in his hand, offering it. When the kid did not take it he dropped it on the ground and began with his own, wadding lengths of paper and sticking them low in the gaps of the pile.

"See, just like this. Simple." he demonstrated.

He offered a sheet to the kid who came forward, took it and rolled it slowly.

"That's it. Just stick it in any nook. Now take another." So the kid took the stack up and assisted slowly. When he had finished he folded his arms and stepped away, like he was ready to relinquish any more responsibility in the operation. But Michael summoned him back. "Take that shovel there and begin digging a ditch around this pile. Work in a circle, starting here. I'll go from the other side."

Michael, taking his, jumped on it into fresh ground, lifting a mound of dirt and emptying it just inside the ring. The kid, given no chance to consider, took the shovel and imitated Michael. Michael went faster first, then the kid caught up. Round they went, rumps bent, heads down. Heaves, stomps. With every chuck of dirt the ordinary languidness on the kid's face was replaced by a rare look of intentness; a firming of his eyes and lips, a strong stiff breath. He squared his body over the ring as he grafted to the work. For those minutes of shoveling, he glowed. While he was still bent over Michael said "Can you douse?"

"Douse?" the kid asked. He stood from his work and when he stood it was like his doubts revived. The firmness left his face.

"I don't know." he continued, "I'm not sure what to do."

"You'll know it when you're doing it." Michael said. "Grab that red gas can and pour it around here," he said. He stopped shoveling and watched the kid go and reluctantly pick it up, holding it away from his body.

"There's a spout. Come over here," he waved. "Take the spout out and pour it on the pile. Be generous."

"Like this." Michael took it once and demonstrated. Then he gave it back. The kid was uneasy but he followed. He looked one last time in the direction of the house, then stepped over the ditch. The spout was a corrugated nozzle and it flowed out freely when he tipped it, and some of the splashing got onto his hands and pants.

"Don't worry." Michael said "That won't hurt you. Keep going."

The kid looked down for something to wipe his hands on.

"Take this." Michael threw him a hand towel, then he kept sprinkling the gas, but tepidly. It made a distinct sound as it drizzled on newspaper; a flat, moist sound; like the first few drops of rain hitting the ground.

"More." Michael said. "Not so careful."

Sprinkling became pouring, but the kid was still too cautious and the pile too big,

"More." he said again, emphatically, and by degrees the kid became more liberal in his pouring

"That's it." Michael said, "Well done." By the end the kid was shaking the canister with abandon; the very act evidently giving him pleasure, for there was a smirk on his face. When he had emptied it in full, the pallets and the couch dripped excess; his hands were cool with the residue of dried gas, and all within the circle was flammable.

"We ready?" Michael said aloud. He tossed the can aside, took a matchbox from his back pocket, crouched and struck it swift, cupping the flame around his hand. He offered it to a piece of rolled newspaper, which caught it quickly and began to burn and spread. He knelt close in fascination, watching how it crept. The kid was beside him. The flame moved along the page with a flossfine embered edge, tattering and nibbling away the page, leaving behind floating, brittle, feather-black ash. The fire in that kneeling corner dwindled, then swelled, then dwindled again, then he blew at it, and a whip of wind kindled it further. It gained life. He blew on it some more and it spread. Michael stood and flicked the match stick into it and stepped back. The kid stepped back with him. Every minute it grew and they stepped back with its pace, watching it grow, until they were beyond the ditch, and the two of them were watching alone.

For minutes there was silence among them. Sizzles and pops. Nightfall. Michael looked at the kid, who had a soft, sad countenance. He stood with his hands on the shovel. Then the pallets caught fire, along with whatever was thrown beneath them; drawers, scrapwood…

Michael requested the shovel from the kid and took it toward the flame, his hands spread wide on the handle, gripping it strong, like he was about to put something out of misery. At the fire's edge he flipped the brown blade over and punched the burning pallets into smaller chunks, then tossed them farther into the pile, making them heap at the base of the stood couch. As he shoveled, the gold necklace dripped off his neck into the blaze light, the physicality of his effort turning his neck and face crimson. Even the gums around his teeth showed the color when he drew his lip up. A vein bulged under his throat. The gold links fell out the shirt buttons, dipping in and out of the light, meddling with the fire, shining, or part of the blaze itself. He took it and put it back into his shirt.

When the cloth of the couch began to burn he dropped the shovel beside him, opened the truck doors and turned on the green backlit dial of the radio, music playing. Behind the radio the door beeped ajar, then stopped. The kid pulled the shovel Michael left lying away from the swelling heat. Then the wind rose. It cut through at random and threw sparks. Michael turned his head away for cover, in the kid's direction. The wind was blowing the kid's hair straight up.

"Here you go, Randy." he said soft to himself. The sky darkened even more. Around them the fields were black; square miles of dark. Straight lines of crops, severe and beautiful. In the distance a door opened. The fire, with its own voice, whelped. It rose, growing into a pillar, tall and unstable, obelisk-like. As it teetered another joined them. Randy's father came from behind, emerging with hardly any notice. He took his hat off and his white combed hair shone in the firelight.

"Good grief." he said quietly, "That's a fire right there." and Michael caught the words and turned in his direction when he spoke. The father's mouth was open slightly- in wonder, in grief, who knew? He was not a man who held his mouth open idly for much.

Michael looked toward the house and saw a figure watching at the window.

"Good for you," the father said in the same flat voice, "nothing grows on that spot anyway." Moments later the couch fell and the high flame with it. It landed with a thud of sighs and a whine of shook metal. Overturned, it burned on its back, smothering the pile beneath and began to put it out slowly. Behind the radio and the sound of fire, another howl.

"Something's out tonight." the father said. "Don't worry about clearing this all tonight. I'll take care of it."

"Are you sure?" Michael said.

"Yes," he said, "I've got nothing better to do."

Michael left the father a shovel and the man stood there alone with it, not moving, not nothing, just watching the fire die. The others stood by the truck. "Close up the back." Michael said to Evan, and the kid did what he was told promptly. Before he did he climbed aboard and swept it clean, and Michael heard him from outside the driver's side, the kid's footsteps followed by the whoosh of bristles. When he was finished he drew down the shambling white door and latched it.

Michael said "Take front."

Michael put the other shovel in the back seat. They got in,

shut the doors, turned off the radio, and left. They drove away slowly. The moon was bright through the windshield and clear enough that they could see the gradations of craters on the surface. The kid, whose clothes had picked up the smell of smoke, sat with his feet crossed, his knees bouncy with the road, and touched his eyes now and then with the tail of his shirt. As they drove away he turned in his seat and saw the father, whose hat was on the ground beside him. The man hovered over the glowing mound, patting down the embers with the back of the shovel. Raking and pushing. Burying.

Turning forward he felt his forehead with the back of his hand. His hands smelled of gas still, a good smell. And now his eyes were heavy with slumber. Michael said,

"There wasn't anything left in the back, was there? I'm sure we emptied it."

And the kid nodded only and answered nothing out loud because he had seen with his own eyes the inside of the truck and swept it and latched the door himself and knew nothing remained. On the main road Michael handed him a few folded bills and there was that understanding between them.

Made in the USA
Columbia, SC
20 February 2023